+
P442b

DEMCO

The
BOLL WEEVIL
EXPRESS

The
BOLL WEEVIL
EXPRESS *a novel*

P.J. Petersen

Delacorte Press/New York

Published by
Delacorte Press
1 Dag Hammarskjold Plaza
New York, N.Y. 10017

Manufactured in the United States of America

First printing

Designed by Richard Oriolo

LIBRARY OF CONGRESS CATALOGING IN PUBLICATION DATA

Petersen, P. J.
The boll weevil express.
Summary: A bored northern California farm boy and a
brother and sister from an orphanage decide to run away
to Idaho but find themselves down and out in San Francisco.
[1. Runaways—Fiction. 2. California—Fiction.]
I. Title.
PZ7.P44197Bo   1983   [Fic]   82–72816
ISBN: 0–440–00856–5

For my mother, who worked at Lytton Home

1

I stood at the side door of the boys' locker room and watched huge raindrops splash into the mud puddles. The rain meant a change in my routine. Usually I got to my world history class by following the dirt service road around the main building. I had to walk farther that way, but it kept me away from the crowds in the corridors. That day, though, the service road was a swamp, and so there was no choice. I had to go through the halls, and I had to go through the old business of walking past people I knew, wondering if they were going to speak to me or not.

Behind me, two guys were having a towel fight. Somebody yelled, "What happened to my shoe?"

I stood in the open doorway and stared out at the storm. The gray skies and the pelting rain suited my mood exactly. I had been depressed all morning, ever since I had realized that the date was February first. A full month of 1957 had gone by, and my life was the same old story—more dull pages out of the same dull book. (Question: What's the shortest book in the world? Answer: *Memorable Moments in the Life of Lars Eric*

Gustafson. Second Question: How did I end up with a name like Lars? Second Answer: Well, my father had a cousin who . . . Just call me Eric and forget it.)

Nineteen fifty-seven was definitely not going according to plan. On New Year's Eve, as I lay in my bed and listened to the radio play the hit songs of 1956, I had made up my mind that my life was going to be different —better. (Remember the old song? "Same old tune but a brand new verse. Gotta get better 'cause it can't get worse.") I had done almost nothing in 1956 but work and go to school. We lived on a dairy farm eight miles from town, and my father traveled those eight miles only when it was absolutely necessary. In the entire year I had been to the movies four times (always with my uncle Charlie, who loved cowboy pictures) and to the Future Farmers' Fair once (with Uncle Charlie again— my father had no use for such things). Otherwise, I had been to two wedding receptions, one Farm Bureau picnic, and a birthday party for my great-aunt. That was it—unless I was going to count funerals. Things had to change. I couldn't stand another year like the last one.

But one month of the new year was already gone, and nothing was different. Every morning of 1957 my father had me up at five o'clock, milking cows. Every afternoon I rode the bus home and worked in the orchards until milking time. Then came the cows. Then dinner. Then homework and bed. Just like 1956 and 1955 and as far back as I cared to remember.

I was still staring at the rain when somebody yelled, "Hey, Stretch, shut that door, will ya? It's freezing in here. I got goose pimples all over my beautiful body."

I stepped back and let the door close, then hurried toward the front entrance, stepping around a wastebasket that had been set under a leak in the roof. The main building, as always, smelled of floor wax and antiseptic. I slipped through the crowd milling around the candy machine and headed down the long corridor. I hadn't been down that hallway for weeks, but nothing had changed. The same old yearbook posters were still on the bulletin boards, and the usual cloud of cigarette smoke was hanging outside the boys' lavatory.

In the crowded hallway I always felt like the new kid in school, even though I knew almost everybody in the place. But people changed when they got to high school, even the people I had known since first grade. Tommy Conte, who had been my best friend through most of grammar school, hung around with other football players and only said hello to me when he was walking by himself. And Paulette Donatelli, who used to stick love notes in my sixth-grade arithmetic book, wouldn't even look at me when she passed by.

I couldn't really blame them. I was the same person, but I looked different. In the past year I had grown nearly a foot without gaining any weight. "Stretch," people called me. Or "Boney Maroney." To make things worse, my clothes came from the local feed store (and looked it), and my lopsided crew cut was obviously a home job. I was a freak, and I knew it. (Step right up, ladies and gentlemen, and see the human toothpick. It's Lars, the man from Mars, in his size thirteen boots.

Watch carefully, though. If he turns sideways, he's almost invisible.)

As I walked into the world history classroom, Denny Shipley was just finishing his daily message. Between classes, Mr. Richards always went down the hall to the janitor's supply room for a quick cigarette. (This was supposed to be a secret, but everybody knew it.) While Mr. Richards was gone, Denny always wrote something on the blackboard. That day he had written, "Kilroy was here but died of boredom."

A stranger was sprawled across the desk directly behind mine. All I could see was the back of a ducktail haircut and a turned-up shirt collar. When I sat down, he began to moan. I turned and looked at him, and he moaned louder. "Are you all right?" I asked.

"Do I look all right, man?" There was a trace of a drawl in his voice, but it was different from any I was used to hearing.

"I don't know. You want me to do something?"

"Yeah, Ace. Get a gun and put me out of my misery."

"What's the matter?"

"I'm dying."

"Oh," I said. I listened to him moan for a minute. "What are you dying of?"

"Hangover, man. The world champion of all hangovers." He lifted his head from the desk and slid down in the seat. He slicked his hair back with his fingers as he looked at me. His face was lean, and his eyes were dark. "Got any cyanide in your pocket?"

"What did you drink, anyway?"

"Two big beautiful fifths of Tennessee bourbon."

"That's a lot," I said. I didn't know anything about liquor, but that seemed a safe enough comment.

"I was still thirsty when I drank the last swallow. If I'd had another fifth, I'd have killed it too."

I watched him run his hands through his hair. "Is this your first day here?"

"Yeah, Ace. Just don't talk so loud, all right? Every sound is like a jackhammer inside my skull."

"Sure," I whispered. "Where you from?"

"Tennessee. Me and Davy Crockett and that whiskey." The tardy bell sounded in the hall, and he clapped his hands over his ears. "What is it, man? A kamikaze attack?"

Mr. Richards came into the room, erased Denny's message, and pulled out his roll book. "We have a new class member," he said, looking back our way. "Stand up and tell us your name and a little bit about yourself. All those girls in the corner are dying to know." Mary Louise Vernon giggled and turned red, the way she always did.

I turned and watched the new fellow pull himself out of his seat. He put his hands on his hips and said, "I'm Doug Walker." He gave a quick nod and continued, "I come from Mission High in Frisco. You probably heard of it. It's the toughest school in the country. Everybody there carries a razor and a zip gun. My English teacher used to carry a loaded forty-five in her purse." He nodded again and started to sit down. "I'm glad to be here."

I had never heard of Mission High, but I was impressed. I did wonder, though, who did the ranking. One of the San Francisco radio stations, KOBY, put together the top forty songs of the week. I tried to picture somebody somewhere counting the number of knifings and making a list of the top forty tough high schools.

"Welcome to Healdsburg," Mr. Richards said. "The only weapon you'll need around here is a club to keep the girls like Mary Louise away." Mary Louise buried her head in her arms.

Soon we were settled into our usual routine of reading the chapter and answering the questions at the end. Mr. Richards found a textbook for Doug, then went back and sat at his desk and read his *Sports Illustrated* magazine. After a while Doug leaned forward and whispered, "Is this it? When are we gonna do something?"

"This is the usual," I told him. "And you don't have to whisper. He doesn't care if we talk, as long as we hold it down. About once a week we have a Mickey Mouse true-and-false test, but that's it."

"You any good in here?"

"There's nothing to it. The tests are really easy."

"You help me out, okay? I gotta get good grades. Good grades and good behavior, and I'll be outa here by Easter."

"What're you talking about?"

"I had a little problem in Frisco, man. Cops stopped me one night just because I had a new set of hubcaps."

"What?" I said.

"Unfortunately, I wasn't in a car at the time. You get the picture?"

"I get it."

"So I got locked up, and they decided that my old lady couldn't handle me. She and my old man are split up, see? So I got sent up here in the weeds, and now I'm Lytton scum. Starting last night."

The Lytton Home for Children, run by the Salvation Army, was three miles north of Healdsburg. Most of the children at the home were younger, but about fifteen high-school-age boys lived there. Some of these may have been orphans, but all of the boys I knew had at least one living parent, who couldn't or wouldn't keep them.

"Is that right?" I said, keeping my face a blank.

"Don't try to fake it. I only came in last night, but I've already heard the whole thing. We're the scum. One of the girls around here starts going with a guy from Lytton, and her folks have kittens—right? We're scum of the earth—right? The Lytton animals."

"Come on," I said. "The guys that say that are the ones that can't get girls. A girl doesn't like a guy because he's a jerk, so the guy says it's because he's from Lytton."

"I couldn't care less, man. I'm not gonna be here long enough for a big-time romance. I'm just putting in time."

I flipped through my book and found answers to the questions. Doug turned pages but didn't write anything. After a while I turned back to him. "Hey, tell me something. How'd you sneak that whiskey into the home?"

Doug looked at me and laughed. "You want something bad enough, you figure out a way."

"So you sneaked in two big bottles of that stuff, and then you drank them, and not one of those guys out there tried to get some of it?"

He laughed again. "Always thinking, aren't you? Any time I'm having trouble on a test, I'll know where to look. You're the guy with all the answers."

At the end of class Doug asked me to show him where the snack bar was, and we walked down the hall together. He marched along as if he owned the place. People looked up as we passed, and several girls who usually ignored me said hello. "What a place," Doug said. "There were more guys in my gym class at Mission than you've got in your whole school. How far is it from here to Frisco, anyway?"

"I don't know for sure. About a hundred miles, I think."

"Man, it seems like a million. This whole place is Marshmallow City. It's a good thing I'm not looking for trouble. I don't think I could find any around here."

There was the usual ridiculous line at the snack bar, but Doug said it was nothing. "Listen, man, in a Mission High line, when a guy cuts in, he's doing it with a knife."

As we worked our way closer to the counter, he reached into his pocket and pulled out a green lunch ticket. "Look at this thing. They don't trust us with money. We have to have tickets instead."

"No big deal," I said. "You get your burger and shake just the same."

"It's just the same as money, huh?"

"Sure."

"Well, then, you use my little green ticket, and I'll use your money."

"It doesn't make any difference."

"I know. So trade with me." I gave him my fifty cents, and he handed me the ticket. We each got a hamburger and milk shake and walked away from the counter.

"See?" I said. "That ticket's no big thing."

"Not to you. Because it doesn't mean anything to you. You're not in jail." We stood at the glass doors and watched the rain come down. "Come on, Ace. Let's get out of here for a while. I want to breathe."

"It's raining," I said.

"You really *are* a smart one. Did you figure that out by yourself, or did somebody help you?"

"It's really coming down. We'll get soaked."

"So what? You've been wet before. Let's take a walk."

We wandered out into the rain. After a block or two, I was wet enough so that the rain didn't bother me anymore. Doug told a long story about a gang fight at Mission High, but I didn't pay much attention. When his story was finished, he turned to me, "You got any gangs around here?"

"Not really. Just some car clubs. Why? You want to start one?"

"Not me, man. I'm a lover, not a fighter." He finished his hamburger and tossed the wrapper into the street. "So tell me, who runs this place?"

"What do you mean?"

"You know, man. Who're the wheels? You?"

"Come on. Do I look like a wheel? You gotta be kidding."

"What are you talking about? You can't tell a wheel by his looks. At Mission the biggest wheel in the place was a guy that had been shot in the face with a shotgun. He looked like something out of a monster movie, but he was smart, and he had class."

"Yeah, but—"

"Hey, man, it's up to you. You're the boss. They can't run over you unless you let 'em. And you didn't seem like the kind of guy that would let 'em. So I figured maybe you're a wheel."

"Come on. I call myself Eric, but I'm the only one who does. You know what the guys call me? I'm Lars, the man from Mars."

He looked over at me and grinned. "That's a good one. Nothing wrong with that."

"It's a joke. Can't you see that? It's a joke, and so am I."

"If that's the way you want it, I guess that's how it'll be."

"It's got nothing to do with what I want."

"Look, you want to be a joke, then you're a joke. You want to be somebody, you can be somebody."

"You sound like the guy in the Charles Atlas muscleman ads."

Doug stretched out his hands as if he were trying to catch the raindrops. "Hey, Lars baby, I'm telling you. It's all in your head."

"Call me Eric, all right?"

"What's wrong with Lars? It's your name, isn't it?"

"Yeah, but I go by Eric."

"Sure you do." He bent down and scooped a handful

of water from the stream in the gutter. He looked over at me, laughed, and then threw the water in my direction. "You know why you go by Eric? 'Cause you're ashamed. There's nothing wrong with being Lars, the man from Mars."

"Lay off me," I said, turning away.

"Hey, Lars, it's not me. It's you. Lay off yourself. You're ashamed of your name, and it's a good name. What do you want to be? Joe or Bill—like everybody else in the world? And you're ashamed of the way you look, and you're one of the biggest guys in school. You wait. In another year you'll weigh two hundred pounds. One of these guys around here gives you trouble, just take down his name. Next year you can get out that list and start knocking heads together." He scooped another handful of water from the gutter and tossed it on me. "Look at the way you walk. You're all scrunched down. You look like a dog waiting to be kicked."

"It's raining."

"You walk the same way in the hall. Come on. Stand up and walk like a man. Show a little class." I straightened my frame a little, not ready to give him too much satisfaction. "Hey, Lars, you're still saying 'Excuse me for being alive' with every step."

"So?"

"So wise up, man. I'm new here, and I need somebody to show me around. Are you gonna do that, or are you ashamed to be seen with Lytton scum?"

"I'll show you around if you want."

"But none of this 'I'm a joke' business. I don't want somebody around that's feeling sorry for himself all the time. I don't mess with losers, Ace. You're looking at Doug Walker, man. Doug Walker—the Tennessee Tornado. We can stand this place on its ear. The Tennessee Tornado and the man from Mars. What do you say?"

I didn't believe it, but when he shoved his wet hand toward me, I shook it. As we made our way back to school, I kept my head upright, looking into the rain.

2

We didn't stand the school on its ear, but things were different around there after Doug arrived. Wherever he and I decided to eat lunch—in the inner courtyard or walking along the streets—we drew a crowd. Doug was always at the center of the group, full of wild stories about zip gun duels and classrooms being set on fire. (My favorite was one about a fellow who gets his thumb sliced off in a knife fight and then carries it in and hands it to the school nurse.)

Now and then I would ask questions, just to stir him up. "Last time you told that, you said the guy's name was Pancho."

"Don't sweat the small stuff, Lars baby."

"Which was it, Pancho or George?"

"Who cares, Ace? The story's true, though. If I'm lyin', I'm dyin'."

"Put me in your will."

But by then he was off on another story. Nobody cared whether the stories were true, anyway. What mattered was that lunch hour was an exciting time, something to look forward to during those dull February mornings.

Every day I rushed through the hallways from my gym class to world history. (You probably figure that I'm going to say that everybody said hello to me now. Wrong. Some did, but Paulette Donatelli was just as stuck-up as ever. One day I told her that I had saved all the love notes she had written me, and then she really made sure she didn't look in my direction. But I loved to walk past her after that.)

One Tuesday I came into history class just as Denny Shipley was finishing his message for the day: "Mr. Richards makes every morning seem like a Monday." Doug was leaning back in his seat with his hands locked behind his head. "It's about time you got here, Lars. I got a surprise for you."

"Don't tell me. You did your own homework for a change."

He sent a kick in my direction. "I said a surprise, not a miracle."

"What is it?"

"Hey, man, I been watching you. You're getting to walk like a person instead of a question mark. So I figure you deserve a reward."

"Whatever it is, I can probably do without it."

"Would I play a dirty trick on you, Lars?"

"Yes."

"You're right, Champ. But not this time. I got you a date."

"Sure you did." I sat down at my desk and pulled my book out of my binder.

Doug leaned forward. "You know Sherry Biasotti? That little dark-haired doll with the dimples?"

"You didn't get me a date with her, and you know it."

"That's right. I figured you'd want your old buddy Doug to have the best, so I get Sherry. You get to have her friend—that little Loretta with those blond curls."

"Oh, sure."

"I kid you not, man. Of course, Sherry's parents won't let her go out on a real date, so we have to meet them at the basketball game. But since we don't have a car, that's not all bad. So what do you say?"

"Loretta? With me?"

"Just say thank you, Lars."

"All right. Thanks. But I don't know if I can make it."

"I can't believe you. I get you a date with a looker like that, and you don't know if you can make it. What do you have going that's better—a hot date with a history book?"

"I live eight miles from here, and I work till about seven every night, and then I don't have a ride or anything."

"Hey, man, figure out something. I just got you a date with one of the best-looking girls around here. You take care of the small stuff, all right?"

I didn't even try to explain to Doug how big the small stuff was. The problem wasn't the time or the distance, anyway; the problem was my father.

All our neighbors referred to my father as Old Hans, even though, at fifty-seven, he was younger than many of them. But when the men around him were leaning against a pickup and talking about the price of hay or the chances of catching a steelhead, my father would be looking at his watch and tapping his foot. "Old Hans," Cap Biancini told me once, "always looks like he just finished eating a pickle."

My father had come to the United States when he was eleven, and he had been working ever since. Because he hadn't had much schooling, he wanted me, his only child, to make the most of my chances. To him, school —like life—was a serious business, and the only out-of-school activity he believed in was homework.

Still, with a chance for a date with Loretta, I decided to give it a try. That night I waited until supper was finished, then caught him before he headed for the parlor and his newspaper. "Father," I said, "would it be all right if I went to the basketball game on Friday night?"

He set down his mug of tea and looked at me. "What?"

I knew that he had heard me, but I repeated my question, adding, "I won't have to go until we finish the chores."

"There's nothing to be gained. You have to get up early for the milking." He pushed his chair back and stood up, always a sign that the discussion was over.

My mother put a warning finger to her lips, but I went on. "I don't mind. I'll get up the same as always. I wouldn't be out really late or anything. It wouldn't hurt anything."

"You'll stay home where you belong," he said, his voice rising. "I know about these things. There's drinking and fighting and racing around in cars. You'll stay home where you belong."

Even as he marched toward the parlor, I tried again. "But I wouldn't be drinking or fighting or anything like that. I'd just go to the game and come right home afterward."

He turned back to me, his face growing red, and pointed a trembling finger in my direction. "No more from you." He stamped into the parlor and banged the door shut.

I looked toward my mother, but she looked away. "It's just a basketball game," I said.

"How come you're interested in basketball all of a sudden?" she asked.

"I just want to go to a game. That's not asking so much, is it?"

"Keep your voice down. There's no sense in making your father angry."

"I don't see what's so bad about wanting to go to a game," I whispered.

"Your father doesn't know about games. He wasn't lucky like you, getting to go to school, never needing anything."

"I know, Mother, but . . ."

"Wait awhile. I'll talk to him. And I'll have your uncle Charlie talk to him." Uncle Charlie was my mother's brother and the only person who could handle my father. Whenever my mother wanted something and my father wouldn't agree, she would get Uncle Charlie to come over. Usually Uncle Charlie could bring my father around, but sometimes it took months.

"Mother, I'm fifteen, not eight. I just want to go to a basketball game."

She shook her head. "You wait awhile. Things will work out."

"You mean to tell me," Doug shouted, "that your old man won't even let you go to a school basketball game?"

"That's right."

"I can't believe it. I got it better than you do, and I'm in that jail out there at Lytton. So what's it gonna be, Lars?"

"What do you mean?"

"Are you gonna keep your date or not?"

"I told you. My old man said I can't go."

"Yeah, baby, I heard you. So what are you gonna do? Here's Loretta waiting for you, and there's your old man. Which way do you go?"

"I can't do it."

"Sure you can—if you really want to. You can't stay out there on that cow farm all your life. Sooner or later you've got to stand up and be counted. It might as well be now, while Loretta's waiting for you."

"I don't know."

"Well, man, you decide. I just got one more thing to tell you. Loretta thinks you're cute, and if you don't do something about it, you're flat crazy."

Knowing that my father wouldn't change his mind, I wondered if it would be possible to go without anybody finding out. On Wednesday and Thursday nights I went upstairs to my bedroom as soon as supper was finished. My room had been made out of part of the attic, so it was well separated from the rest of the house. Both nights I closed my door tight and stuffed a towel underneath to be sure that no light would show. Then I waited to see what would happen. On either night I could have been gone, and nobody would have known. I decided it was worth the gamble.

Friday night I left the supper table and hurried upstairs. The game started at eight o'clock, which left me only forty minutes. I changed my clothes in a rush, shut my door quietly, flipped off the light, and went out the window. In less than a minute I was across the roof and down the cypress tree at the corner of the house.

Once I had crept away from the front yard, I trotted down the narrow lane to the county road. Then I slowed to a walk. It was eight miles to town. Even for Loretta, I couldn't walk that far. I had to wait and hope for a ride.

Hitchhiking was a risky business for me. Few people traveled that road after dark, and I couldn't be sure that anybody would come by. But that was only half the problem. Almost anybody who did come by was likely to know my parents. My father had lived in the valley for nearly twenty years, and my mother had been born there. The first time I spotted a pair of headlights, I didn't know whether to be glad or not.

A rattling old Ford passed me without slowing down. Then, fifty yards down the road, brakes squealed as the car skidded to a stop. The door opened, and somebody yelled, "That you, Lars?"

I ran up to the car and saw Wilbur Patterson wave me inside. "Where you headed, boy?"

"Healdsburg. There's a basketball game tonight."

"That's great. Who're you playing?"

I told him, and we talked about school and fishing and the weather all the way to town. He dropped me off in front of the gym, even though it was out of his way.

"Thanks a lot," I said as I opened the squeaking car door.

"You betcha, Lars. One thing, boy—does Old Hans know you're here?"

"No."

"I didn't figure he did. Have a good time, boy."

The night was perfect. Healdsburg won the game on a last-second shot, Loretta and I held hands most of the second half, and Doug found somebody who would take me home if I'd toss in a dollar for gas money. But all through the evening I felt uneasy, as if someone were standing behind me.

I walked down the lane to my house, climbed the cypress tree, and crept across the roof to my bedroom window. The only sounds came from the barns, where the cows were moving around, the way they always did. I lifted the window gently and straddled the sill.

The bedroom light snapped on, and my father grabbed the front of my jacket. "So that's the kind of boy you are," he shouted. "Sneaking into your own house like a burglar. That's the way you are, huh? You sneak and lie like trash." He threw me against the wall. I hit solidly and let myself slip to the floor. "I'll fix you. From now on, you'll be too busy to get in trouble. You just wait." He stood over me, as if he expected me to say something. I lay in the same spot and stared at the floor. "What do you have to say for yourself? Huh? What do you have to say?" I shook my head. "Nothing? Nothing big and smart?" I shook my head again. "You make me sick. Lousy sneaking trash." He stamped out of my room and down the stairs.

I never did know how my father found out. Wilbur Patterson may have called him, or Wilbur may have told somebody else, or it may have been a pure and simple accident. However it happened, I was up at four thirty Saturday morning, and I was kept busy until long after dark. Sunday was the same.

On Monday I told Doug the whole thing. "Well, Ace," he said, "you made one mistake."

"Only one?"

"Yep. You shoulda kissed Loretta good night. You had a good dark half a block between the gym lights and where Sherry's father had parked the car."

"Come on. How would that have kept me out of trouble?"

"It wouldn't, man, but you shoulda done it, anyway. If you'd kissed her, at least you'd have had something nice to think about at four thirty in the morning."

3

For three weeks nothing changed at home. I was kept busy every minute I wasn't at school. (Question: What's worse than spending Saturday working for fifteen hours around cow barns? Answer: Spending Saturday working for fifteen hours around cow barns when you know you'll get another fifteen hours on Sunday.)

Each night my father came up the stairs, opened my bedroom door, and looked inside. He never said a word. He just glared at me and then turned away.

The first time I caught my mother alone, I asked her how long she figured this routine was going to last. "You're doing fine, Lars," she said. "Just stick to it. It won't last too much longer."

"It's not fair."

"You disobeyed your father, and he's very angry." And that was it, except that she said she'd get Uncle Charlie to come around once things had settled down. That didn't do much to raise my spirits.

At school, some things changed. Loretta went to the next basketball game with somebody else, and Doug set up dates for himself and two other guys. "I can get you one, too, Lars," he said. "Just say the word."

"I can't make it."

"You ever think about going on strike? Why don't you go out there in that barn and sit down and not move? Tell your old man that Abraham Lincoln already freed the slaves."

"Oh, sure."

"Listen, they'll keep dishing it out as long as you keep lapping it up. Haven't you figured that out by now?"

"It's not that easy. My father lives in his own world."

"Well, it's time somebody blasted him out of it. Just tell him you have some rights, too."

"If you know all the answers, how come you're always copying my homework?"

"Okay, Ace. I won't say any more. You already know I'm right anyway."

The days pressed down on me. After supper I went straight to my room and then ended up staring out the window into the dark. None of my books kept my attention, and the radio only reminded me of the world that was out of my reach.

School kept me going. During the lunch hour on Tuesdays and Thursdays, the Girls' Athletic Association had field hockey games. Doug rounded up a whole group of boys for a cheering section and then led yells. ("Healdsburg apples. Petaluma eggs. Cheryl's team has gorgeous legs.") Nobody had ever paid any attention to

G.A.A. games before. The girls were a little embarrassed at first, but they got used to the attention before long.

One noon in early March, Doug led a couple of cheers and then motioned for me to walk down the sideline with him. The others started to follow, but Doug stopped them. "You guys stay here and cheer for that cute little goalie. I gotta talk to the man from Mars about something." As we walked away from the others, he said, "I had a nightmare last night. Terrible. Woke up screaming. I dreamed I lived my whole life in Healdsburg. It just about scared me to death."

"That's bad," I said, still watching the game.

"Guess what, man? I got grounded last night. No games, no movies, no television. For two weeks I'm in the same shape you are, except that I don't have to get up and milk some dumb cows. But I can't leave the home except to go to school."

"What did you do?"

"I was insolent. That's what they called it, anyway. You know what that means? It means I told this old lady to take a flying leap. Then I was supposed to go back and apologize, and I was insolent again. That's what cost me the extra week."

"I'd still trade you." I turned away from him and yelled "Good play" at Cheryl Bartlett, who had just tripped somebody with her stick.

"I've been thinking, Ace. You're stuck out there on that cow farm, and now I'm stuck at Lytton. I figure it's time for you and me to take a ride on the Boll Weevil Express."

"What are you talking about?"

He laughed. "That's something my daddy used to say. There was a song he used to sing to us about the boll weevil, this little bug that was looking all over, trying to find a home. So whenever Daddy'd get sick of where we were living, he'd say, 'It's about time for a ride on the Boll Weevil Express.' And off we'd go again, looking for a new place. I figure it's about time for you and me to do the same."

"Where would we go?"

"What difference does it make? You name it—it's gotta be better."

"Yeah, but—"

"What would you say to a place where you could fish any time you wanted? Big trees. Lots of room. Nobody crowding you. But plenty going on at night—every night, if you wanted."

"Sounds all right, but you have to die before you can go to heaven."

"It just sounds like heaven compared to this place. I'm talking about Idaho. My old man's up there, at a place called Twin Falls. There are lots of jobs around there. We could get jobs and rent us a house and be out on our own. No more of this jailhouse stuff. We could do anything we felt like."

"Still sounds like heaven to me."

"Well, Lars, it's out there waiting for us. Let's go."

"Sure. Right now, huh? Or are you going to wait until the hockey game is over?"

"Listen, man, we have to make some plans and get things together, but we can be ready in a few days."

I turned and looked at him. "Are you serious?"

"Dead serious, man. I've had it with Lytton. I've been cool out there, playing it straight. I figured I could take whatever they were dishing out and get out quick. Now I find out it doesn't matter. There's no getting out. Not for me, anyway."

"What do you mean?"

"I'm just there. Period. I'll be there till I finish high school or till you and I go to Idaho. They have custody of me. You know, like your mother and father. And I can't take it. Everything there's on a schedule. If I want to know where I'll be at six thirty next Tuesday, all I have to do is check the schedule. I can't live that way, Ace. If I have to stand in another line, I think I'll explode. I'm sick of cooperating, and I'm sick of being polite to people who keep fussing at me. Some guys are just born insolent, man. And I'm one of 'em. So I got to thinking—why don't you and me just check out of this place? Good riddance, Healdsburg. Adios, Lytton. Goodbye to those dumb cows. What do you say?"

I looked out toward the field, where the teams were gathering for their end-of-the-game cheers. "It sounds good, but . . ."

"Don't start that stuff. Either come with me or don't. Take your choice. But don't start in with a bunch of excuses. If you want to go, that's cool. If you're chicken, that's cool, too. But don't start in telling me how neat it is around here."

"Don't worry."

"Well, what do you say? Is it time for the man from Mars to see what the rest of the world looks like?

Huh? You ready for a ride on the Boll Weevil Express?"

"I'm ready," I said, sounding more certain than I felt.

"Well, then, look out, Twin Falls—we're headed your way."

We spent a week planning our escape. We went to the school library and read about Idaho. We got out maps and traced our route, studying each choice carefully. ("Stay away from those big highways, man. That's where all the cops hang out. And see that big brown spot? That's desert. So let's cut up north of that.")

I began selling things to raise money—my old baseball mitt, a hunting knife, a sterling silver belt buckle, even my radio. Meanwhile, Doug made list after list of things we should take, always insisting that everything we carried should fit into our pockets. ("If the cops see guys like us with a bedroll or a suitcase, they know we're running away. But if they just see a couple of guys walking down the street, they won't pay any attention.")

In spite of all the lists and planning, our strategy was very simple. I would come to Lytton Home in the middle of the night. From there we would hitchhike to San Francisco, where Doug would get some money from his mother. Then we would take a bus from San Francisco part way to Idaho—far enough to get us out of danger. Then we would hitch rides the rest of the way.

Actually, the plan wasn't quite that simple. Doug had another wrinkle in mind, but I didn't know it then.

While I worked in the barns, I went over each detail. (Should we go through Reno or Alturas? Should we bring fishing line and hooks, or should we wait and buy them in Idaho? Should I wear my oxfords or my sneakers?) I checked out books on Idaho and read them far into the night. I kept scrounging things to sell. I even tried to memorize maps so that we wouldn't have to carry one, but I gave that up after three nights and three headaches.

Meanwhile, Doug was getting anxious. "Look," he finally told me, "it's time to move. I got problems at the home, and I'd better clear out while I still can. Let's hit the road."

"When?"

"Good question, Ace. What do you think? Maybe next week? The week after that? Maybe next month? You'd like that, wouldn't you? You could just plan and plan for a whole month."

"I just asked when."

"Tonight's the night. Tonight I'm gone. If you want to come, you be at the Lytton gates at midnight. If you chicken out, then you deserve all the boring times you have on that cow farm. I'll send you a postcard from Idaho."

"I'll see you at midnight," I said, wondering if I really meant it.

I might not have gone if Notto Cavalo hadn't died that night. When I came home from school, Uncle Charlie was just climbing into his pickup. "Hey, Lars," he yelled, "you been to any basketball games lately?" He howled with laughter and pounded on the pickup door. "I been telling your old man that this is California, not

Siberia. Now he's mad at both of us. Just now he told
me to get off his property and never come back. Heck,
boy, it's been almost a year since he ran me off." He
laughed and started the engine. "Tell your mother good-
bye for me. I had to leave in a hurry. Old Hans was
ready to dig out his shotgun. Bye, Lars. Don't do anything I wouldn't do."

This kind of fight was always a hopeful sign in our
family. In a few days Uncle Charlie would send over a
piece of blue cheese or a smoked eel. ("Squarehead
food" he called it.) Then a few days after that he would
show up, and they would talk some more and probably
have another argument. When my mother wanted to get
her kitchen remodeled, this went on for six months, but
usually things moved faster than that.

All through the milking I tried to make up my mind. I
wanted to leave, but the thought of going somewhere
new scared me. I had spent my whole life on that dairy,
and I could count the number of times I hadn't slept in
my own bed. The more I thought, the more confused I
became. Idaho seemed a million miles away. And what
if we were caught? And what about school? If Uncle
Charlie could get my father to ease up a little, maybe
things wouldn't be so bad at home.

When I sat down to supper, I still wasn't sure what to
do. Then the telephone rang, and somebody told my
mother that Renato Cavalo had just died of a heart
attack. The news stunned me.

Notto was a cranky old man who lived two miles
down the road from us. Once in a while, on Saturdays, I
worked for him. He always managed to cheat me a little

on my hours, but he sent me home with his old *Alaska Sportsman* magazines. "That's the place, Larsy," he would say. "That's where I'm going one of these days. The rest of the world—New York, Italy—let somebody else go. But I'm going to see Alaska before I die."

And now he was dead, and he'd never see Alaska. He had lived over sixty years in one spot and had never done the one thing he wanted to do. I could see a clear lesson in all this. Life didn't stand still, even if people did. If I stood still, the way I had been doing, life would rush past me, just the way it had rushed by Notto.

My course was clear; I was leaving that night.

As soon as supper was over, I mumbled something about homework and went upstairs to my room, where I finished all my preparations in ten minutes. I wasn't really hurrying, but when you're only taking what you can fit into your pockets, packing doesn't take long.

I wished I had a different jacket, although I had saved for six months to buy that one—a red letterman's job with leather sleeves and slant pockets. But the pockets were better suited for my hands than for anything else. Even the few items I had—socks, underclothes, a map —created suspicious bulges.

The only thing on my list that I didn't have was a flashlight. We always had three or four around the house —all with dead batteries. There was no point in looking for one. I didn't have room for it, anyway.

All I had left to do was to write a note to my parents. But that turned out to be even harder than I figured. In one or two starts, I tried to explain why I was going, but nothing came out right. Then I sat and stared out the window into the darkness, trying to think of the right words. I tried to imagine sitting down and telling them what I had to say, but that didn't work either. I couldn't get past the first sentence. All I could think of was my father standing up and marching out of the room.

Just after nine, while I was still staring at a blank page, my father came up the stairs, looked in my door, and turned away. "Father," I said quickly.

"What?" His answer was too fast for me. I tried to think of what I had intended to say, but nothing came. I just stared at the empty paper. "What is it?"

I had to swallow before I managed to ask, "What time is Notto's funeral?"

"I don't know yet." I listened to his feet clump down the stairs.

Time kept slipping by, and I couldn't think of any-thing to write. I knew that I had to hurry, but that only made things worse. (Should I write "Dear Mother and Father," or should I just start the note? What if I didn't leave a note at all? What about just writing "Good-bye"?)

Finally, anxious to get started, I scrawled, "I'm going somewhere to get a job. Please don't worry about me. I'll write when I can." I wasn't satisfied, but I didn't think that the next one would be any better. I scrawled my name at the bottom and left the note on my pillow.

4

It was ten fifteen when I climbed down the cypress tree. That left me an hour and forty-five minutes to walk the six miles to Lytton—plenty of time, by my calculations. After all, an ordinary walker could make three miles an hour, and I was in a hurry.

The night was dark, though, and the road was full of chuckholes, and every dog in the valley wanted a piece of my hide. (Question: Which are worse, big dogs that race out ready to go for your jugular vein or little dogs that sneak up behind you and try to amputate your foot? Answer: Whichever ones are after you at the moment.) Even when my night vision was at its best, I was lucky to avoid wandering off the pavement. And every few minutes a car or a rattling pickup would come along, and I would have to dash away from the road and lie in the grass until it passed.

By eleven o'clock I was a mile behind schedule. I shoved my hands into my bulging pockets and started to run. Then the dogs really wanted me.

When I reached Highway 101, I slowed to a walk for

the final hundred yards and tried to catch my breath. A car came by, but I just stayed on the shoulder of the highway. It was too much trouble to hide.

Doug stepped out from behind a pillar as I approached the gates of the home. "Hey, Ace, I was about to give up on you."

"I'm here," I managed to say.

"You sound like you're dying."

"You run six miles and see how you sound."

"You got all the stuff?"

"Just about. I couldn't get a flashlight."

"No problem. We'll pick one up in Frisco. Got plenty of bread?"

"About forty bucks."

"Forty? That's it, huh?"

"Don't start that stuff. I sold everything I had to get that much."

"Was I complaining, Ace? We can do it on forty." He grabbed my arm and yanked me back against a concrete pillar. "Quiet," he whispered. "Somebody's coming."

I flattened my body against the pillar and tried to look into the darkness. I held my hands in front of my mouth to muffle the sound of my panting.

"Douglas?" a girl's voice whispered. "Douglas?"

"I can't believe this," Doug said, stepping away from the pillar. "Cindy, what are you doing here?"

I watched a figure come out of the darkness and move up close to Doug. "I'm not gonna stand for it," she said. "I thought about it, and I'm not gonna stand for it. You're not gonna go off somewhere and leave me here, not knowing whatever happened to you."

"Come on, Cindy. I told you not to worry. I'll be all right, and I'll write to you just as soon as I can."

"Big deal. I've heard that one before, and so have you."

"I'm talking straight," Doug said. "I'll let you know where I am."

"What is all this?" I asked, finally in control of my breathing. "Who's she, anyway?"

"No problem, Lars," Doug said. "We'll go right now. Look, Cindy, I have to get moving."

"Stop right there," she ordered, her voice far too loud. "If you take one more step, I'll start screaming. I'll have the whole home out here before you get to the top of the hill."

Doug laughed. "Come on. I wouldn't have told you I was going if I'd known you were gonna be like this."

"I mean it, Douglas. Stay right where you are."

By this time I was really angry. I could just see our whole plan being wrecked because Doug told some stupid girl about it. "What in the heck is going on?" I said.

"Don't get excited, Lars," Doug said. "She doesn't mean it."

"Oh, yeah?" she said. "You just keep thinking that, and you'll get a real surprise."

"Look, Doug," I said, "it's almost twelve thirty. We've gotta get started or forget it. Get rid of her, and let's go."

"Why don't you put an egg in your shoe and beat it?" she said. "This is between my brother and me."

"Your brother?"

"That's right. My brother. He's all the family I got. That'll show you how hard up I am. And now he's getting set to run off and leave me."

That was enough for me. "Forget it," I told Doug. "You two go ahead and have your family fight. When you decide you want to go somewhere, you let me know." I turned and walked away from the gates.

"Hold on, Lars," Doug said. "Just give me half a minute. I'm ready to take off."

"Oh, sure," I said, still moving as I spoke. "And we get about a hundred yards down the way, and she'll have the whole crew after you. Forget it."

"That's right," she said, walking along beside us. "Even this dummy has it figured out, Douglas. So use your head. It's just plain stupid to go running off this way."

"I don't care," Doug said quickly. "I'm going all the same. Even if you yell, I'm going. If I get caught tonight, then I'll try it again tomorrow night. And the night after that. I've had it with this place."

"Oh, that's just dandy," I said. "Maybe you think it'll be a big joke to get caught before we start, but I don't. Forget it. You and your sister get everything settled. Then, if she'll give you permission, maybe we can go somewhere. For tonight, I'm going home." I began walking even faster.

"I hope you don't think I'm not glad to see you go," Cindy called, "because I am. Good riddance."

"I'll tell you one thing," I said over my shoulder. "I'm not sorry I never had a sister."

"Go crawl back in your hole," she said.

Doug trotted up beside me and caught my arm. "Hold on, Lars."

"Let go of me," I said.

"Hey, man, you don't need to get excited. We're going tonight. I won't let you down. Just give me a minute, okay? I'll take care of her right now, and then we'll go." He tapped my arm and headed back toward his sister.

"Make it quick," I said, following after him. "If we're not going, I have a long walk back home."

"I'm not staying here," Doug told her. "There's no way you can make me. You can get me into trouble, but you can't make me stay."

"I know it, you feeble-brained baboon. You never did know when you were well off. Here you are with three meals a day and a place to sleep and a chance to go to school, and you can't wait to go somewhere else where things will be worse. You can't stand it till you end up hungry and cold again."

"I don't care. I'm not staying here any longer."

"I figured as much," Cindy said disgustedly. "I just knew you'd blow this one. I wasn't even gonna argue with you, but I figured I oughta give it a shot. But I knew you'd be too pigheaded to listen. That's why I brought along my stuff. Might as well talk to a wall as try to get you to listen to sense."

"What do you mean you brought along your stuff?"

"You know cottonpickin' well what I mean. I've got my pockets full and my purse stuffed tight. If you're leaving, so am I. There's no way I'm staying here while you're out doing who knows what. You're a sorry enough specimen, but you're all the family I got left."

Doug started to say something, but she cut him off. "If you can't find 'em, you can't count 'em for family, and that just leaves you. So I'm not letting you go off too."

"No way," I said. "I don't want anything to do with this."

"If you think we'll take you along, you're crazy," Doug told her.

I turned and started for home. "Forget it," I said over my shoulder. "I'll see you at school tomorrow, Doug. Nice running away with you."

Again Doug came running after me, but I ignored him. "Hold it, will ya, Champ?" When I kept walking, he ran directly in front of me and stopped. I tried to push him aside, but he caught my arm. "Don't get excited, man. Just give me a minute."

"I already did—about three times." I tried to pull free from him.

"I don't care what you morons decide," Cindy said, coming up behind us. "If Douglas goes, I go."

"Hey, Lars," Doug muttered to me, "stay with me, all right? We'll let her come along tonight. We'll hitch a ride to Frisco. Then we'll leave her with my old lady. I'll get my money, just the way we figured, and we'll head out. It's just for a few hours, just long enough to get us to Frisco. By morning we'll be right where we figured to be."

"This whole thing is crazy," I said. "I don't want anything to do with it."

"Come on, Lars. We're gonna have some fun. Stay with me, man. The man from Mars and the Tennessee Tornado—look out, Idaho. We're headed your way."

"Oh, sure. With your sister tagging along behind."

"Don't worry, Lars. Everybody gets a little scared now and then. So what? So you spilled a little mustard down your back. It's okay. Little yellow streak coming out? That's cool. You'll be all right in a while."

I pushed him to the side. "Lay off that stuff. I came like I said I would. And you don't see *my* sister standing here."

"And this time tomorrow you won't see mine either. Come on, Lars. It's just for tonight. Trust me."

"I might puke," Cindy said. "Anybody stupid enough to trust you deserves whatever he gets."

Doug punched me on the arm. "Let's go, Champ. We've wasted too much time already."

I didn't know what to do. I hated the idea of taking the girl with us, but after making my decision to leave, I also hated the idea of going back home.

While I stood and tried to decide, Cindy stepped between Doug and me. "What's the matter with you, anyway?" She moved up close to me and looked up into my face. The top of her head came only to my chest. "It's hard to tell in the dark. Do you look as dumb as you act? Even a moron should know better than to run off with a Lytton kid. When a Lytton guy goes, the cops are on his tail right away. Didn't you know that?"

"Hey, Doug," I said, "call off the dog, will ya?" I looked down at her. "How old are you?"

"What do you care? It happens that I'm almost fourteen, and I already know more than you ever will. I'm pretty good-looking too, but you better not get any ideas. You try anything with me, and you'll wish you'd stayed home with your mommy."

"Don't worry," I told her. "The less I have to do with you, the better I'll like it."

"Why not start now, you clod? Just get out of here. Go back home to your cage."

"Shut up, Cindy," Doug said. "Lars, you're with me, okay? We'll make it."

I knew it was crazy to leave with the two of them, but right then I couldn't face the walk home. "If we're going, let's go," I said, moving to the shoulder of the highway. "There's a car coming right now."

"Hey, man, you can't do that."

"You got a better way to hitch a ride?"

"Hey, think about it, Ace. A guy comes along, sees the sign for the Salvation Army home, then sees us standing here with our thumbs out—you think he's gonna stop? He'll stop, all right. He'll stop in Healdsburg and call the cops."

"You got it all figured out," I said. "You tell me how we're supposed to get to San Francisco—fly?"

"Take it easy, Lars. We'll head down the highway, keeping away from the cars. We'll scoot around the edge of Healdsburg and then hitch a ride when we get on the far side."

"Just what I need," I said. "More walking."

We hurried along the shoulder of the road, moving back whenever headlights approached. At the outskirts of Healdsburg, we cut away from the main highway and followed the back streets. All the houses were dark, and even the dogs seemed to be asleep.

We were in the middle of an especially quiet block when Doug whispered, "All right, Ace. You had enough walking?"

"Oh, man, I've been a long ways tonight."

"All right, then. It's time we hitched a ride."

"Oh, sure. With all this traffic, we can't miss."

"No problem. We'll just do a little Mission High hitchhiking. How's this one look?" He started toward a white Ford that was sitting at the curb just ahead of us.

"Oh, no, you don't!" Cindy shouted. "Not on your life!"

"Quiet," Doug whispered, waving his hands.

"Forget it, Douglas," Cindy said, lowering her voice a little. "If you think I'm gonna let you steal a car, you're out of your mind."

"Don't start that kind of stuff," Doug said. "It's getting late. We can pick up a car here, drive to Frisco, and be rid of it before anybody knows it's gone. No problems. No sweat. We'll just borrow it for a little while."

"Not on your life," Cindy said, her voice bouncing off the houses around us.

I felt like hitting both of them. "Cut it out," I said. "First thing you know, we'll have somebody calling the cops."

"Let's move on," Doug said. We hurried along for a few blocks before he said anything more. Then he moved up between Cindy and me and whispered, "What time is it?"

"Just after two," I told him.

"See? It'll take another half hour to get out of town. What kind of chance do you think we'll have of catching a ride at two thirty in the morning?"

"Forget it right now, Douglas," Cindy said. "If you want to go to reform school, that's up to you, but I won't let you take me with you. Once we get to San Francisco, you're on your own. But I'm not gonna ride in a stolen car, so just drop the whole dumb idea."

"Look," Doug said, "it's the only chance we got."

"Hey, what is this?" I asked him. "I thought we had this whole thing planned out. You never said anything about taking a car."

"Relax, Ace. I just didn't want you worrying about the details ahead of time. I knew you'd come around when the time came."

Cindy stepped in front of me and looked up into my face. I had to stop walking to keep from running into her. "Are you getting the picture, clod? He's a liar. He always has been. He had it figured all along to steal a car, but he didn't bother to tell you. And you're so dumb, you'd go along with it. Where'd he find you, anyway?"

I was too disgusted to answer. If I had had time to get back home before my father woke up, I would have left the two of them right then.

"Let's keep moving," Doug said. "You've already made enough noise to wake the dead."

We walked for several more blocks without talking. I was too tired and too disgusted to have any ideas. I just kept plodding along, wishing that things were different.

Doug put his arm around my shoulder and whispered something that I didn't understand, but I didn't bother to say anything. He left me and moved next to Cindy. "Look, I can hotwire one of these, and we can take it a few miles. Just far enough to get us clear of Healdsburg. We don't have to take it all the way to Frisco."

"Forget it."

"Come on. You're as tired as I am. You don't want us to get into trouble, do you? We've got to get out of this place."

"Douglas, I'm not even going to answer you anymore."

"I've had it," Doug said. "That car up there—the blue one—that's the one I'm taking. It's the kind of car nobody ever notices. Just a plain old Chevy. We'll just take it a few miles down the road and leave it."

I was in a kind of daze by then. I didn't want to take a car, but I was so tired that nothing seemed to matter. My father was going to find my note in two hours, and I was still in Healdsburg.

Doug trotted ahead of us. "Door's not even locked," he whispered. He moved around the car and slid into the driver's seat. I stood on the sidewalk and watched his head disappear beneath the dashboard.

Then Cindy screamed—a short, piercing shriek, as if she had been stabbed. I turned toward her, expecting to find her crumpling to the sidewalk. She was standing with her hands on her hips. "You want to hear another one?" she whispered.

A light came on in the window of a house across the street. "Forget it," I said, and walked away quickly. I glanced around me, but no other lights came on. Doug was out of the car and onto the sidewalk before I reached the end of the block. Cindy moved along beside him.

I kept ahead of them for five or six blocks. Plodding along the sidewalk, I tried to think of some way out of the fix, but nothing came.

"Hey, Ace, wait up," Doug called after a while.

As disgusted as I was with both of them, I couldn't see much choice. I stopped beside a picket fence and squatted down. My knees were so shaky that I almost fell.

"Why didn't you just keep moving?" Cindy said as she came close. "We have problems enough without a big clod like you tagging along. Where'd you dig him up, Douglas? Old Clodhopper Jones—straight off the farm."

"Shut up," Doug told her. "Hey, Lars, we'll forget about taking a car. We'll head out of town here and see if we can pick up a ride. There's no use trying to talk sense to her."

Cindy snorted. "You finally figured that out, did you? You're so dumb—if I wasn't related to you, I wouldn't even talk to you."

It was well past three o'clock when we crossed the bridge that led out of Healdsburg. We were ready to try hitchhiking, but the highway was deserted except for a few diesel rigs.

As we walked along, Doug tried to get a story straight, in case a cop stopped. "It's getting toward morning. We can tell him that we're on our way to Santa Rosa to check on jobs. They start interviewing at eight, and we want to be first in line."

"Fantastic," Cindy said. "What job? Or don't you think he'll ask that?"

"I don't know. Any job. Maybe a restaurant. How's that sound, Lars?"

"I don't care," I mumbled. That was the truth. If a policeman came by, I didn't plan to stay around long enough to answer any questions.

"Good luck," Cindy told him. "You couldn't lie your way out of a phone booth."

"We'll say there's a new restaurant opening," Doug said.

"I hope we don't get stopped," Cindy moaned. "I'd hate to try to explain what I was doing with two morons like you."

We walked, and we walked. Toward morning a few cars began to appear, but nobody even slowed down. It grew light enough so that we didn't have to worry about stumbling into chuckholes, and soon we could see the drivers who passed us. Usually they were men wearing silver hardhats or baseball caps—men on their way to work somewhere.

"Listen," I said finally, "we're in trouble. By this time my old man knows that I'm gone. We probably have the cops after us already."

"Maybe not," Cindy said. "Are you sure he wants you back?"

"Lay off," Doug told her. "If it hadn't been for you,

Lars and I would be in Frisco right now. We've had a bad run here, but we're still all right. We're away from Healdsburg at least. All we have to do is lay low for a while."

"Where?" Cindy asked.

"No problem. We'll find a place if we have to. But maybe we'll get lucky and catch a ride."

We didn't get lucky. At six thirty we left the highway, crossed a field, and slipped into an old weatherbeaten shed. There was nothing inside but a few pieces of farm equipment—rusty plows and a cultivator—scattered across the dirt floor.

"Perfect," Doug said. "Just what the doctor ordered. We'll get some sleep, and then we'll take off this afternoon. The best time for hitching is right after school is out." He sat down in an open spot between two old tractor tires. "It looks like things are starting to turn our way."

"Terrific," Cindy said. "Hey, Clodhopper, did you bring anything to eat?"

"No," I told her. "We didn't figure on this."

"You didn't figure—period. I should have known. Anybody dumb enough to run off with Douglas is too dumb to remember that he has to eat in the morning."

I huddled on the damp dirt floor and thought of bacon frying. Then it hit me that I would never taste my mother's cooking again. I pictured her the way I saw her every morning, bent over the stove as she shouted, "Anybody hungry?" I wondered what she was doing right then. Would she go ahead and cook breakfast, or would she just sit on her stool in the corner of the kitchen, the way she did the day my grandfather died? I rolled over and tried to think of something else, but that picture of my mother on her stool kept coming back to me.

5

I woke up stiff and sore, with my face in the dirt. Sunlight was pouring through the cracks on the other side of the shed. Cindy sat and watched me as I tried to brush the dust off my clothes. I was surprised to see how small and young-looking she was. I guess I hadn't really looked at her the night before. Her blond hair was tangled, and there was a muddy streak across her forehead, but she had the kind of round face and blue eyes that you see in magazine ads. If I hadn't known what a pain she was, I might have fallen in love with her right on the spot.

She put a finger on her lips and walked over to me. "I need to talk to you," she whispered.

I nodded and stretched. One of my legs was asleep, and I rubbed it and kicked the ground as the feeling began to return. "Oh, brother," I muttered.

Cindy sat down across from me and looked up into my face. Her eyes were a darker blue than I first thought. They seemed too old for the rest of her. "You feel pretty good, huh?"

"You bet," I said. "Like I've been run over by a truck."

"You had enough of this?"

"I'm okay."

"Sure you are."

"I wasn't complaining. I'm just a little stiff, that's all."

"And you're all set and ready for more, I suppose?"

"I'm okay," I said again.

"All that business last night didn't wise you up?"

"What do you mean?"

"What do you need, to get hit by lightning? Here's Douglas and his fantastic plan. He just doesn't happen to tell you that he figures to swipe a car first chance he gets. Doesn't that tell you something? If you had any sense at all, you'd cut and run while you still can. This is a sinking ship, and it's time for the rats to head out."

"You really know how to start a guy's day off right," I said, looking away from her.

"Look around you. You walked all night, and where are you? You're in some dumb farmer's barn just outside of Healdsburg, and you haven't had anything to eat for a day. You look like a hobo already, and you're so sore you can hardly move. How much of this kind of fun can you stand?"

I stood up slowly and began to work my stiff joints. "I feel like an elephant stepped on me." I walked over and stared out through the cracks. Cars sped by on the highway, making a hissing sound as they passed.

"You look like it too." Cindy came and stood behind

me and began to brush my hair with her fingers. "Bend
over so I can reach you. Your hair's full of dirt, and it's
all matted down. Look, why don't you go back home?
Things are only gonna get worse, and you know it.
Down deep, you know it. You're in with a loser."

I turned around and looked at her. "I can't go back.
Even if I wanted to, I can't."

"Why not?"

I looked back toward the wall. "I don't want to talk
about it."

"That's what people always say when they know
they're wrong."

Doug groaned and sat up. "All right," he shouted,
"you can bring me my breakfast now." He let out a
crazy laugh.

"You can have mine," I said. "I'm not hungry."

He stretched out one arm and rubbed it with his other
hand. "I've slept in better places in my life." He looked
over at me. "I don't know what you were thinking
about, Lars. You should have had sense enough to bring
along some blankets."

"Don't give me that. You said we'd get spotted as
runaways right off if we were carrying bedrolls."

He laughed again. "It's still your fault. Next time
don't listen to me. What do I know about it?"

"Nothing," Cindy said. "Nothing at all." She walked
back to where she had been sleeping. "I don't suppose
either one of you brought along a mirror?" Nobody said
anything. "I don't know why I even bothered to ask."

Doug brought a comb out of his pocket and started on
his hair. "I don't know about you two, but I've had

about as much of this place as I need." He stopped and held up his hand. "What's that, anyway?" He turned away from us and walked around the cultivator to the far side of the shed. He looked through a crack and yelled, "Gangbusters!"

"What is it?" I asked him.

"Grab your stuff, and let's move."

"What're you talking about?" Cindy asked, standing in the same spot.

"There's a freight train just stopping across the way. And right up the line is a big old empty boxcar with our name on it. Let's move."

We scooped up our things and dashed out the door of the shed. I glanced once at the highway behind us, then lowered my head and ran through the orchard toward the open boxcar.

I had never ridden on a train. In fact, the only times I was ever around trains was when my grammar school pal Louie Buzzini and I used to stand in his backyard and wave at the engineers as the slow-moving freights pulled away from the station. Once, while we stood counting cars, we had seen a man standing in the doorway of a boxcar. He had taken off his old hat and bowed to us. Now it was my turn.

Doug scrambled up the embankment first and pulled himself into the car. I was right behind him, anxious to make it up without any help. The car was bigger inside than I thought it would be. When the cars had rolled past Louie Buzzini and me, they hadn't seemed especially large. This one, though, was enormous, almost as big as a schoolroom.

"Well, give me a little help, for heaven's sake," Cindy said. Doug and I reached down, caught her hands, and pulled her up. She stepped past us and looked around. "What a mess!"

She was right. The floor was splintered planks, and the paint on the metal walls was flaking and peeling. I wasn't worried about looks, though. I had just hopped a freight.

"We'd better get away from the door," Doug said. "Somebody might come by."

We hurried to one end of the car and crouched in the corner, waiting for the train to start moving. I bounced on the balls of my feet, too excited to stay still.

"What's the matter with you?" Cindy asked. "You look like you got the itch."

"Let's get going," Doug muttered. "Come on, baby. Let's put it in gear and move."

Five minutes went by. Then five more. I began to wonder if there was something wrong with the train, but I didn't dare say anything.

"Listen," Cindy said. "I couldn't see either end of this thing. Are you sure it's headed in the right direction?"

"Come on," Doug said. "I saw it pull up and stop. It's headed south, all right. I'm not about to get us on a train going in the wrong direction. How stupid do you think I am, anyway?"

"I won't answer that," Cindy said.

Then there was a rumble, and the floor beneath us jerked and jerked again. "Here we go," I said. "We're on our way. San Francisco, here we come."

Doug grinned at me. "Man, when I was talking about

riding on the Boll Weevil Express, I didn't know we'd get the real thing."

"How am I gonna sit down without getting my rump full of splinters?" Cindy demanded. "Douglas, let me use your coat."

"Use your own."

I hurried back to the open doorway and held on to the doorframe while I watched our shed slide past. I danced from one foot to the other, loving the feel of the floor moving beneath me.

The train slowed and slowed, and I suddenly wondered if somebody had spotted us. Then there was a crash, and the car yanked to a stop. I grabbed the wall to keep from falling. "We hit something!" I shouted.

Doug looked over at me and grinned. "Easy, Ace. They're just hooking up to something."

"That's what I meant."

Cindy snorted. "Sure it is, Clodhopper Jones. You want to let me use your jacket?"

"Why should I?"

"No reason. Not unless you wanted to show some manners or something. I guess you never heard of things like manners out on the farm, did you?"

"Lay off him," Doug said.

"Don't worry about me." I unsnapped my jacket. "If you want it, you can have it." I pulled my arms out of the sleeves and carried it to her. "Just be careful of the stuff in the pockets."

She took the jacket, dropped it onto the floor, and sat down quickly. I stood and watched her for a minute, expecting her to say something. When nothing came, I went back to the doorway and stared out. "What's taking so long?"

"You didn't have to give her your jacket," Doug said. "She could have used her own if she wanted to sit down."

"Go take a long walk off a short pier," Cindy said.

The train lurched twice and then began to creep in the other direction. "How come we're backing up?" I asked.

"Just relax," Doug said. "They're just getting cars hooked up. No need to get excited."

I stood beside the doorway and watched the orchards creep by until our shed came into sight again. "How far are they going to back up, anyway?"

"Take it easy, man. They've only gone a little way. We'll stop any second now."

But there was a funny note in his voice. Outside the car, the orchards were passing by faster than before, and the noise of the wheels was growing louder and louder.

"Hey," I said, "are you sure—"

"We'll stop any second," Doug said. "Just don't get excited. It's got to stop." He stared out at the orchards, which kept slipping past a little faster and a little faster. "It's got to stop. It's *got* to!"

Cindy jumped up and ran toward the doorway. "Don't tell me," she shouted. She looked out for a second, then screamed, "I can't stand it!" She turned and pounded on Doug's arm, as if she were driving a nail. "You idiot! You stupid, lying idiot!"

"It wasn't my fault," Doug shouted back. "I saw the dumb train going south. Maybe it's—"

"Maybe nothing," Cindy said. "You've done it again, you idiot."

By then, the orchards we passed were just blurs of trees. Far ahead of us, the whistle of the engine sounded.

Cindy stamped back and sat down on my jacket again. "Terrific," she shouted. "We'll be in Healdsburg in no time. Hey, Douglas, maybe if we're really lucky, it'll stop at Lytton and save us all that walking."

"I didn't know," Doug said to me. "I saw it headed south, and I saw it stop. I didn't see the front of the train, but what was I supposed to think? Come on, Ace. It wasn't my fault."

"What difference does it make?" I said, leaning out of the doorway so that I could look ahead. "I just hope it doesn't stop right in the middle of Healdsburg."

"Don't sweat it," Doug said. "If we get picked up, you can tell everybody we went to Frisco and then came back on the train."

"That'll make my father really happy, all right."

"Don't worry, man. We won't get picked up. But don't stand there in the doorway and advertise."

I moved back and crouched in the corner as we passed the Healdsburg depot without slowing down. As soon as I was sure that we weren't stopping, I let out the breath I had been holding and made my way back to the door. The town looked different from the railroad tracks. The same buildings that were sparkling white in front had boarded-up windows and rusty fire escapes facing the tracks. Seeing the house where Louie Buzzini used to live made me wish that there had been some boys out in the yard for me to wave to.

The train was moving at a steady clip when it passed Lytton. Doug shook his fist and yelled something, but I couldn't hear what.

After we passed the next town, Geyserville, I found a fairly smooth plank and sat down to watch the view. I didn't know where we were going, and I had no idea when the train would stop, but at least we were going somewhere.

"This is just great," Cindy yelled. "You dummies want to go to San Francisco, so you hop a train to Oregon."

"Drop dead," Doug shouted back. "It was a mistake, all right? It could have happened to anybody."

"To anybody really dumb," Cindy said.

"We're all right," I yelled.

Cindy waved me away. "Sure we are, Clodhopper. And when you start getting hungry, you can eat all that food that you were smart enough to bring along."

I leaned back and ignored her. The railroad was following the river, and I knew that there were tunnels up ahead. I could eat anytime, but how often did I get to go through tunnels?

The train sped past the Cloverdale depot while we stood back from the doorway. Then we were back along the river and plunging into our first tunnel. "Wow!" I shouted before the noise and smell got to me. (Question: What's it like inside a tunnel? Answer: Dark and damp and noisy. Like being in an old musty cellar while people with sledgehammers pound on metal barrels— only worse.)

Before long I would have traded all the tunnels in the

world for a hamburger. I moved over next to Cindy, who pretended not to notice me. "I need my jacket now," I told her. "I'm just about to freeze to death."

"No loss."

"Come on. I let you have it as long as I could. Now I need it back."

Cindy stood up slowly, straightened her skirt carefully, and then kicked the jacket toward me. "Go ahead and take it. What do you care if I have to stand up from here on?"

I pulled on my coat and fastened the snaps. "Thanks," I told her.

"What's the matter with you? What are you doing thanking me for giving you your own jacket?"

I grinned at her. "I was just trying to teach you manners. I guess you never heard of things like manners in Tennessee."

She tried to glare at me, then turned away when she started to smile.

In the next hour two more towns—Hopland and then Ukiah—zipped past us. I didn't know what to expect after that. I had never been that far north before. We passed through tree-covered hills, and the air turned even colder. I sat and tried to get comfortable, while my teeth hammered together.

"This Boll Weevil Express is a whole lot of fun," Cindy shouted. She was sitting down too. She had stood and complained for a while after I took my jacket back, but she finally gave up and sat down on her purse. (And complained some more.)

"Just shut up," Doug yelled back. "We didn't want you to come. We'd have been in Frisco last night if it hadn't been for you. So don't start in on me. I'm sick of listening to you."

"Touchy, touchy," Cindy said, but she didn't keep it up.

When the train began to slow down, we stood up and hurried to the doorway. "This is it!" Doug yelled. "Get ready to jump. We're gonna starve to death if we don't get off of here."

I was ready to follow him whenever he decided to jump. Right then I couldn't think of anything worse than staying in that boxcar. But the train slowed and slowed, and the wheels shrieked and moaned as we rattled to a stop. Doug stuck out his head, then yelled, "Let's go!" He leaped out, and Cindy and I swung down beside him.

The three of us dashed across an open grassy area into a thicket of scrub oaks and manzanita. Huddling behind a stand of trees, we peered back at the train. Nobody was in sight. "Made it," Doug said and sank down onto the ground.

"Made it where?" Cindy asked. "Just tell me where we are, all right?"

"A long way from Lytton. Lay off me. As soon as the train goes on, we'll go up the tracks to the town. We don't want anybody to spot us now."

The section of the train where our boxcar sat didn't move, but we could hear the engine far ahead, adding or unhooking cars. "Come on," I kept mumbling. "Get that thing out of here."

It was nearly dark when we watched the caboose go past. By that time we could see the lights of the town ahead of us. "I don't care what kind of town this is," Doug said. "They've got to have something to eat here."

6

We discovered from the sign on the depot that we were in the town of Willits. I had never been to Willits before, but judging by what I could see, I hadn't missed anything. The old white houses, the trees next to the sidewalk, even the dogs—the whole place looked like Healdsburg to me.

We headed down the street next to the depot, moving toward the brightest lights. In a block or two we came to Highway 101. I stood and looked at the sign, feeling better somehow. No matter how hungry and tired I was, at least I wasn't lost.

"Just think," Cindy said. "All we have to do is walk down this road for a hundred miles or so, and we can be right back where we started from."

A few blocks south we found a hamburger stand. All three of us stood and stared at the painted sign that was the menu. I wanted everything on the sign. A tired-looking woman stood and tapped her pencil on the counter while we kept staring.

"Come on," Doug said finally. "Let's order some hamburgers while we're trying to decide."

We ordered six hamburgers and then studied the sign while the woman tossed the patties on the grill. When she brought our burgers to the window, I paid her and ordered milk shakes and chili dogs.

We sat at a picnic table and ate. And ate. French fries, onion rings, corn dogs, turnovers. Every few minutes one of us would trot up to the window and order something else. When I finally ordered ice cream cones to carry away with us, the woman just laughed and wouldn't let me pay for them. "These ice creams are on me," she said. "I just hope you all don't get sick."

We walked along under the streetlights and ate our cones. We were headed south, but I hadn't even thought about what would come next. Right then it was enough just to be full.

"Oh, baby," Doug groaned, "I feel like I swallowed a cannonball. It's all your fault, Lars. You were the one that got us started eating chili. My stomach's never gonna be the same."

"One of you want this ice cream?" Cindy asked. "I think I'm through." She tossed her cone into a vacant lot when neither of us said anything.

"Good idea," Doug said, throwing his into the grass. My cone was growing soggy, but I kept nibbling at it as we walked. "What are you trying to do, Lars? Make that thing last until breakfast?"

Just as I started to answer him, a police car suddenly passed us and turned into a driveway, blocking the sidewalk in front of us. The driver opened the door quickly and motioned for us to come forward. We waited on the sidewalk while he walked slowly around his car. I could feel the ice cream dribbling onto my hand. I was too scared and sick to think of eating any more, but I didn't dare throw away the cone with him right there.

The policeman was short and round-faced, with dark wavy hair that glistened under the streetlights. He stopped at the curb and looked each of us in the eye. "Okay, kiddos," he said finally, "what's the story?"

I stood and stared at him. By this time my hand was covered with ice cream. I held my arm away from my body so that the ice cream wouldn't drip on my pants.

"Just walking home," Doug said. "Walking along, not doing a thing wrong."

"Good for you, kiddo. Just walking home and keeping your noses clean, right?"

"Yessir."

"Tell you what. I'm just roaming around tonight. Hop in, and I'll give you a ride home."

For a minute I thought Doug was going to try to bluff it. He even took a step toward the car before he said, "The thing of it is, sir, we don't live right here in town."

The policeman smiled for the first time. "The thing of it is, I already knew that. I saw you coming up the tracks awhile ago. So, tell me, what's the story with you?" He looked over at me. "You always eat ice cream that way?"

I tried to think of something to say, but ended up shaking my head.

"Go ahead and throw it in the gutter. Go ahead. I promise not to arrest you for littering." I dropped the cone and tried to scrape the mess off my hands.

"You see, officer—" Doug started.

"I've heard enough from you, kiddo. You go stand by the front of the car and wait. And take your girl friend with you. I want to talk to the Ice Cream Kid here." He walked up beside me and said, "Come on, buddy." I followed him into the street, where he stopped and rested one foot on the rear bumper of the car. I glanced sideways to make sure that Doug and Cindy were still there. "Don't look at them. This is just you and me. I want you to give it to me straight. No smart talk. No bull." He handed me a Kleenex from his back pocket, and I used it to wipe off my hands.

"Thank you."

"No problem. Now, where you from?"

"Cloverdale," I said, surprising myself with such a quick lie.

"What're you doing here?"

"We didn't plan on coming here. The dumb train never stopped."

He laughed as he pulled at his collar. "Is that right?"

"We were just messing around this afternoon," I said, raising my voice to be sure that Doug and Cindy could hear me. "We saw this open boxcar just sitting there, and we decided to take a little ride. We were gonna jump off in a minute or so, but the train got going too fast, and we had to stay on. And then it didn't stop anywhere. It kept going right through all the towns until it got here. We thought it was never gonna stop."

He laughed again. "So you kids got a little more ride than you bargained for, huh? And now you're headed back to Cloverdale. You don't think you want to take the train, huh?"

"I don't ever want to ride on a train again," I said, telling the absolute truth.

He reached out and caught my shoulder. "So you were messing around and hopped a train and ended up in Willits, huh?" I felt his hand clamp down on my shoulder. "What's in your pockets?"

I looked down at the bulges in my jacket. The tail of a T-shirt was hanging out. "Bunch of junk."

"Like what, kiddo?" His grip on my shoulder tightened.

"Bunch of junk from my gym locker," I said. "Like this old shirt." I held up the shirt tail, then stuffed it back.

He let go of my shoulder and straightened his tie. "Tell you what I'm going to do, buddy. I'm going to take you back to the station, and we'll call your parents, and somebody can drive up here and get you."

Before I could think of anything to say, Cindy was running toward us. "Don't do that, sir!" she shouted. "Oh, please, don't do that! My father will kill me. If he finds out I was on that train and all that, he'll beat me to death. I swear he will. If you call him up, he'll come here and be nice as pie. Then he'll take me home and kill me. He really will."

The policeman rocked back on his heels and yanked at his tie again. "Maybe it isn't as bad as all that."

Doug came up closer. He seemed about to say something, but he didn't come out with it.

"You don't know my father," Cindy said. "He's not like other people. He goes crazy when something like this happens."

"He doesn't sound too different to me," the policeman said.

"Look here," Cindy said. "I'll show you how different he is." She reached up and unfastened the top button on her blouse.

"Hey, hold it. What do you think you're doing?"

"Take it easy," Cindy told him. "I'm not about to take off my clothes here in the middle of town. I just want to show you." Reaching behind her head, she pulled her coat and blouse away from the back of her neck. "Maybe when you see the scars, you'll believe it. Come here and look."

"Never mind," the policeman said, stepping back.

"I can't even show you the real ones," Cindy said, "but they're there."

"I believe you, kiddo." His voice was quieter than before.

"You want to see my brother's? He's got some good ones too."

"Never mind," he said, turning back to me. "That's your sister, huh?"

"Not him," Cindy said. "That idiot back there."

"What about you, buddy?" the policeman said to me. "Couldn't your parents come up and get you?"

"Oh, sure," Cindy said. "His father might come, but somebody'll have to sober him up first."

"Look, officer," Doug said, "we aren't gonna cause any trouble. We just want to hitch a ride back home."

The policeman looked at us and shook his head. "I'll tell you what. I get off work a little after eleven. I'll give you a ride down to Cloverdale then."

I started to say something, but Cindy drowned me out, saying, "Oh, gee, thank you. That's really nice."

"Hop in the car. I'll take you over to the station. You can wait there until I get off. We've even got a television for you to watch."

Cindy headed straight for the car door, saying, "Gee, this is really nice of you. I really appreciate it." She opened the door and put one foot inside. "What time is it, anyway?"

"About eight thirty," the policeman said.

"You know, I was just thinking. We might be smarter to stay here and try to catch a ride. If we could get home earlier, it might make things better." She stepped out of the car again.

"You don't want a ride, huh?" The policeman was looking us over again.

"It's not that," Cindy said. "It's just that we're already in trouble, and the longer we're gone, the worse it'll be." She turned around and hit Doug on the shoulder. "You moron. You knew all about it, didn't you? Nothing to be scared of. We'd just climb on and ride a little ways. I should have known better than to listen to you." She punched him again.

"I'll tell you what. I think we better . . ." He stopped talking to listen to a call coming over his radio. I couldn't understand what the voice said, except that part of it was numbers. The policeman trotted to his car. "I'll be back in a few minutes," he shouted.

He slammed the door, and the siren began. The tires spun as he backed onto the street, then raced to the north. We stood on the sidewalk and watched the red lights grow smaller and smaller.

"All right," Cindy said, "let's make ourselves scarce. There's no telling how long he'll be gone."

"Let's go," I said and began to run.

"Hold it, Clodhopper," she shouted. I stopped and waited for them. "That's all we need—to have somebody tell him that we went running off down the road. Just settle down and walk naturally, but keep it moving."

We didn't say anything more until we were beyond the last streetlight. I looked back toward Willits and said, "You did really good, Cindy."

"So did you," she said disgustedly. "Aren't we terrific? Two liars and an idiot. What an outfit!"

7

A half mile past the City Limits sign we stopped in the middle of a straight stretch of road and waited for a ride. A cold wind brought fog over the mountains to block out what little moonlight we had. We huddled together on the ground, one of us standing up whenever headlights came our way. (Question: How can you tell if a driver spots you when you're hitchhiking at night? Answer: Easy. He speeds up.)

I held out as long as I could, waiting for one of them to say something. After all, my jacket was heavier than either of theirs. But when I couldn't hold my jaw tight enough to keep my teeth from chattering, I stood up. "Let's go back to Willits. Something's bound to be open."

"Yeah," Doug said. "The police station."

I began to do jumping jacks. "We can't stay here all night. We'll freeze to death."

Doug stood up and shadowboxed around me, tapping my arm once or twice. "Come on, Champ. It's a little rough right now, but we'll make it. Tomorrow night you'll be sleeping in a bed in Frisco. Then Idaho, here we come." He punched my arm harder. "We're gonna do it, Lars. We've had a bad run, but we're not finished. We're not gonna quit the first time things get rough."

"Oh, save it," Cindy moaned. "Next thing you'll be saying is 'Let's win one for the Dipper.' Or is it Gipper? Skipper?"

"Don't pay any attention to her," Doug said.

"Hey, Clodhopper," Cindy said, "what's the name of that movie—you know, with all that Notre Dame football junk?"

"I don't know. I never saw it."

"How could you miss it? It's on TV about once a week. We've already seen it twice since we came to Lytton."

"We don't have a television," I said.

"What? You're kidding."

"No. Our house is in a bad location. There's a mountain or something in the way. We can't get any reception at all. I don't think my father would have bought one, anyway."

Cindy stood up and brushed off her skirt. "No wonder you're running away. You live on a boring farm out in the country from a boring town, and you don't even have a TV. Anything would look good to you, even running away with a moron."

We walked up and down, stamping our feet. I tried a few more jumping jacks, but they made me tired without getting me very warm. When headlights appeared, Doug moved out onto the highway. "This one's mine. I'm gonna flag him down. When he stops, I'll tell him that one of you is sick or something."

"What a fantastic plan," Cindy muttered as she and I moved back away from the road. "Listen, Clodhopper, you ought to get smart and go back to Willits on your own. This whole thing is crazy. You're supposed to go to Idaho where Daddy is, right?"

"I guess so."

"Maybe before you go too far, you ought to ask Douglas how long it's been since he heard from Daddy. And have him tell you what a neat guy Daddy is."

"What are you saying? If you got something to say, come out and say it."

"It's a fairy tale, stupid. Don't you know that by now? If you have any sense at all, you'll go back and call your parents. You won't even get in trouble. Nobody knows you ran off with us."

"Forget it," I said. "I can't go back home."

"Why not? What's stopping you?"

"I just can't. Now leave me alone."

The car slowed as its headlights picked up Doug. He moved farther out into the road, waving his arms. The car sounded its horn and swerved into the other lane as it moved past. "Dumb Willits hillbillies," Doug yelled.

"You can go home any time you want to," Cindy said. "And your mother will be so glad to see you . . ."

"Lay off, will you?" I stood up and moved back to the highway. "Hey, Doug, how do you turn off that machine back there?"

"Cut it out, Cindy," he yelled. "This whole thing's your fault anyway. If you hadn't been such a creep, we'd have taken that Chevy and been in Frisco last night.

And right now the smart thing would be for me to slip back into Willits and pick up a car."

"Don't start that again," Cindy shouted.

"Aw, can it, will ya?" Doug told her. "I said that would be the smart thing to do. But with you along, we'll do the dumb thing. We'll just walk. This is Highway 101, so every step we take gets us that much closer to Frisco, and we might pick up a ride any time. And I don't want to hear you complain, Cindy, because you made the choice." He rubbed his hands together and suddenly laughed. "Hey, we're all right. We slept all day, and we had plenty to eat. All we have to do is stay warm. Let's move out."

We walked single file down the middle of the road, trying to keep the white line between our feet. When a car came past, we moved to the side of the road and stuck out our thumbs, but we didn't have much hope. Once in a while we would spot a light far off to the side, or we would hear a dog bark. Most of the time, though, we seemed to be the only three beings left in the world.

Around midnight a car with a single headlight came toward us, moving more slowly than the other cars had. We stood on the shoulder of the road and held our thumbs high. The car rattled past us, slowing even more.

The brake lights flashed as the car pulled toward the side of the road. "I knew our luck had to change," Doug said, trotting forward. "Here we go."

The car creaked to a stop about fifty yards ahead of us. As we ran that way, the door on the passenger side opened, and a man yelled, "You guys tired of walking?"

"We sure are," I yelled.

"Well, then, you better run awhile." He cackled, and the door slammed, and the car's motor roared. Its tires spun in the gravel, spraying us with pebbles and dirt.

Doug heaved a rock in that direction, but it fell far short. The three of us stood in the road for a while without saying anything. Then Cindy snorted and said, "You knew our luck had to change, didn't you?"

"Don't start in," Doug said. "Just don't start in."

We walked for another hour before we decided that we were more tired than cold. We made our way to a thicket that would cut the wind and then huddled together on the ground. Cindy pushed up against me, and I could feel her arms shaking. "You had your chance to get away, and you muffed it." She burrowed close to me and tucked her hand beneath my arm. "Don't get any ideas. Right now I'm so cold I'd snuggle up to a dead horse if I thought it would help."

I sat there, my teeth clenched, and wondered if I was ever going to be warm again. I decided that if I ever did this again, I was going to take some blankets, no matter what anybody said.

I was positive that I'd never be able to sleep that way, but I woke up with the sun in my eyes. (Question: How does a person feel after sleeping under a tree on a cold March night? Answer: You don't want to know.)

Doug and Cindy were already up and moving around. I got to my feet and tried to slap the dirt off my clothes. "You better let me try hitching," Cindy said. "You two stay back out of sight. The way you two look, anybody crazy enough to stop for you is too crazy for us to ride with."

"You're not gonna win any beauty prizes yourself," Doug told her. "At least comb your hair. It's all mashed down on this side."

Cindy took a comb from her pocket and went to work. "This running away is sure lots of fun. You guys know all the neat places to stay, too."

"This is gonna be a good day," Doug said. "I got the old feeling back. Today's gonna be the start of good things."

"It better hurry," I said, watching the first three cars rush past Cindy.

"Stick out your thumb," Doug yelled at her. "How're they gonna know you want a ride?"

"Before you start giving advice, Dougie, you better remember how you've been doing. Just think about all the neat places we've slept in and all the fun times we've had."

"I'm just telling you, they're not gonna know you want a ride if you don't stick out your thumb."

"Your brain froze last night. Look, a pretty girl is standing by the road looking pitiful. Do you think she'll get a ride faster if she sticks out her thumb like some skaggy tramp?"

"You're doing great so far," Doug said.

A white sedan, traveling well over the speed limit, slowed just as it passed Cindy. Then the tires squealed as the car skidded to the side of the road. I started forward, but Doug caught my arm. "Don't show yourself yet. The guy might take off." The car backed up, bouncing along the shoulder of the road. Cindy reached down and picked up her purse.

The door on the passenger side swung open, and a man's voice called out, "You need a ride?"

"I sure do," Cindy said, walking slowly to the door. "I thought nobody would ever stop."

Doug crept forward, bending low enough that his head wouldn't show above the windows. He pushed Cindy toward the open door and stood up as he grabbed the handle of the rear door. "Boy, mister, thanks a lot for stopping."

"Where'd you come from?" the driver asked. Cindy was inside the car as I came forward. "Hey, what is this, anyway?"

"Give us a break," Cindy said. "Here we are in the middle of nowhere, and these hillbillies won't ever stop."

The man was about forty with a moustache that looked as if it had been penciled on. He looked at Doug and me and shook his head. "Forget it, kids. I just saw the girl by the side of the road and pulled over to help. I'm not the Greyhound bus."

"Give us a break," Cindy said. "Just give us a ride to the next town before we starve to death out here."

"What's it gonna hurt?" Doug asked. "We're stuck out here in the weeds. How about it? How about giving us a ride?"

"Brush yourselves off good," the man said. "I don't want you messing up my seats. What did you do—sleep by the side of the road all night?"

Cindy settled herself in the front seat and slammed

the door. "If we did, it wasn't our fault. Do you think we'd be hanging around a place like this if we had a choice?"

"You've got a point there, kid." He watched Doug and me climb into the back seat and close the door.

"All set, mister," Doug said when we had sat for a minute.

"Mister Wilkins to you, sonny boy." He looked at each of us. "Now, before we move, I want to know what I'm in for. What are you kids up to? You running away from home or what?"

"The thing of it is, Mr. Wilkins—" Doug started.

"It's no use," Cindy said. "I confess. I'm a dangerous bankrobber, and there's a posse with bloodhounds on our tail. And if you don't hurry up and go, you'll end up with dog hair and blood all over your car."

Wilkins laughed and put the car in gear. "I figured you looked like a desperate character."

"You're just lucky I wasted all my bullets on the posse," Cindy said.

"This must be my lucky day, all right." He didn't say anything more until we were on the highway, doing about seventy miles an hour. "One thing I want to get straight, kids. If there's any trouble, I don't know a thing about it. I just saw some pitiful kids alongside the road, and I gave them a ride. I didn't ask any questions, and you didn't volunteer any answers."

"Good deal," Doug said.

"How far you kids going?"

"Frisco."

"Say San Francisco, boy. Only people that don't know any better say Frisco."

"He doesn't know any better," Cindy said.

"Me," Wilkins announced, "I'm going to San Jose. I have an appointment with a crook this afternoon." He went on and told about how he had gotten the best of this fellow the last time they got together. His story was all about percentages and discounts. I didn't understand it, but I think I laughed in the right places. When Doug heard me laugh, he chimed in, too, even though he had been dozing the whole time.

"It's only eight o'clock in the morning," Wilkins said after a time, "and I feel like I've already put in a day's work. I came all the way from Eureka this morning. What do you think about that?"

"That's a long way," I said when nobody else answered him.

"You better believe it, especially with all the fog I hit up north. I was up at four this morning. Four o'clock!"

"Four, huh?" I said because he seemed to expect an answer.

"That's right. I hardly knew what to do with myself. I figure the only way to look at four in the morning is from the long side—stay up that late if you're having fun. It's sure no time to be getting up in the morning, that's for sure. But it's a crazy world, and you have to go where the money's being made."

The car was warm, even a little stuffy. I lay back against the seat and felt my legs and arms begin to relax.

Cindy was lying against the door, and Doug had slid down in the seat.

Wilkins laughed as if one of us had told a joke. "This is a real live-wire outfit. If I picked you up for company, I made a real mistake."

8

The first thing I heard was the car door opening. I looked up as Wilkins stepped out onto the pavement and stretched his arms above his head. "Are we in San Francisco?" I asked.

He laughed. "Not exactly. When you wake up and look around, you'll see what a dumb question that was. No, this is some podunk town. But I gotta get some coffee. I'm about to fall asleep. If you three hadn't been snoring so loud, I probably would have. You want to come along and get something?"

"That's great," Cindy said, sitting up and looking around.

I started to say something as I reached for the door handle, but my mouth and my hand stopped at the same moment. Looking back through the rear window, I could see a traffic light and the park beyond. I glanced to my right and saw the neon signs of the Sportsman's Club and, beyond that, the back end of the funeral parlor. "I'm not hungry," I managed to say as I slid down in the seat.

"Are you kidding me?" Doug said. He opened the

door of the car and stepped out into the street. He ran his fingers through his hair as he waited for a car to pass.

"I'll buy you something," Wilkins said, "but if you start ordering T-bone steaks, you're on your own."

"Doug," I whispered. "Doug!"

He leaned back into the car. "What's the matter with you?"

"Don't you know where you are? This is Healdsburg."

He laughed. "Hey, you're right."

"I can't go anywhere," I said, sliding farther into the corner. "Half the people around here know me."

"Well, I'll bring you something." He slammed the door and dashed across the street to catch up with Wilkins.

I scrunched down in the back seat so that my head was below the rear window. I turned my wrist so that I could see my watch and count the minutes.

Before long, I moved around so that I could see the tops of the buildings across the street. Then, when there was a lull in the traffic, I sat up enough to see the service station that was just ahead of our parking space. The attendant—a guy named Ernie—was sitting in the office reading a newspaper. And on the near side of the drive-way, just a few steps from the car, stood a telephone booth.

I watched Ernie and the traffic and that booth for several minutes, although I had already decided to call my mother. She was a worrier, the kind that always thinks the worst. I figured I could at least call her and say that I was all right. First, though, I had to get my plan straight. (Would she know who it was right away,

or should I say, "Hello, Mother, this is Lars"? I decided
on just "Hello, Mother." But then what? What did I
have to say to her? I couldn't tell her the truth—that I
was in Healdsburg—but I didn't want to lie.) I finally
decided to tell her that I was fine and that she shouldn't
worry. Then I would hang up before she had a chance to
ask questions.

I waited until the street was empty and walked
quickly to the booth. Pulling the door closed, I dropped
the dime and then couldn't reach down and get it without opening the door again. I glanced quickly at the
service station, then. shoved open the door and grabbed
the coin. Banging the door shut, I pushed the dime into
the slot and dialed quickly, thankful not to get a busy
signal. While the rings sounded in my ear, I recited,
"Hello, Mother. I just wanted to tell you that I'm okay
and not to worry."

"Hello," a woman's voice boomed. I didn't recognize
it.

"H-hello. Is Mrs. Gustafson there?"

"No, she isn't here right now. This is Lars, isn't it?"

I thought about lying but decided there was nothing to
be gained. "Yes," I admitted.

"Well, Lars, your mom went to a funeral this morning. She left a little while ago. This is Ada Tankersley.
Your mom let me come over here and do my washing.
My machine's been busted for two weeks now, and that
lazy Wilbur Bates still hasn't been out to fix it. He says
he can't fix it until a part comes in, but I know better'n
that. How does he know which part I need when he
hasn't laid eyes on the machine?" While Mrs. Tankers-

ley went on about Wilbur Bates, I was wondering
whether she had heard about me. I knew my parents
would call the police, but I didn't know whether they
would tell anybody else or not. My father wouldn't—I
knew that—but my mother would tell her family right
away, especially Uncle Charlie. And once the news got
that far, it would probably spread quickly.

"Look, Mrs. Tankersley," I interrupted, "could you
give my mother a message for me?"

"Well, all right, I guess. Just hold on a minute while I
try to find a pencil." She dropped the receiver against
something hard. I stood with my back to the street,
hunched over as far as I could. Somebody I didn't know
pulled into the service station, and Ernie set down his
paper and came outside. I could hear Mrs. Tankersley
humming. "Hey, Lars, do you know where your mom
keeps her pencils? I can't seem to find anything here but
an old ball point that doesn't write."

"Look, Mrs. Tankersley, it's not that big a message.
Just tell her I called and that I'm okay."

"Don't you have school this week, Lars? It's not vaca-
tion time or anything, is it?"

"Just tell her, would you please, Mrs. Tankersley?"

"You'll probably see her before I do. I just have one
more load to run. I'm going to take them home and hang
them on my line, so I'll be gone before they get back.
They're going to Notto Cavalo's funeral, see, and that'll
take an hour or more. And then I think your dad wanted
to get some things at the feed store."

"Listen, it's important. Will you call my mother and
give her the message?"

"You mean you want me to call up your mother just to tell her that you're okay? Is there something funny going on? Your mom was acting kind of strange this morning. I thought maybe she didn't like me asking to use her machine."

"Look, Mrs. Tankersley, write her a note or call her. But tell her, will you? It's important."

"Well, all right. If you say so." She paused for a minute. "You're not doing something weird, are you, Lars?"

I didn't know how to answer that. As I glanced to the side of the service station, I saw Uncle Charlie marching up the street toward the phone booth. I bent over the telephone with my back to the street, expecting to hear Uncle Charlie bellow at any moment. Meanwhile, Mrs. Tankersley was saying, "I can't hear you, Lars." When I was sure that Uncle Charlie had gone past, I hung up the receiver.

As I turned to look at the sidewalk again, the whole area was crawling with people I knew. The Danheusens were parking their red pickup across the street, and old Ben Hillford was putting money in a meter just beyond.

I glanced at the sidewalk quickly, saw that it was empty on my side of the street, and crawled from the booth to the car. I could only hope that Ernie wouldn't look in my direction. I flung open the back door of the car, dove inside, and yanked the door closed. Feeling too exposed on the seat, I scooted down onto the floor. I lay there on my stomach with my knees bent, my feet sticking up in the air. (My shoes were still below the window, though, so I hoped they wouldn't be noticed.) I wished desperately for some kind of cover—a blanket or even a coat. But the back seat was empty except for a brochure for vacuum cleaners. Without thinking through any of my actions, I grabbed the brochure, tore out pages, and put them over the top of my head. (Question: What would people think if they saw me there, jammed in between the seats, with pieces of paper sliding off my head? Answer: They'd figure somebody had a screw loose—and they'd be right.)

Outside the car everyone I knew was walking along the sidewalk. Familiar voices called back and forth.

"Hey, Kelley, how's that well coming?"

"Aw, next time I'll dig it myself with a shovel. I'd get done faster. Pastori's rig breaks down every time somebody sneezes."

"Lot of people here."

"You going to the cemetery afterward? Helen said we ought to stop by her house for something to eat before we head back home."

"Who's looking after Notto's animals?"

"Glen's been doing it up till now, but he's getting tired of it. He figures those cousins of Notto's can figure out what to do."

"I hear Notto didn't have a will."

"He prob'ly didn't. He always said he didn't care what happened after he died. Said his cousins could cut each other's throats over the place, as far as he was concerned."

It was the kind of talk I had heard all my life. When

one of the valley people died, the farmers came to pay their respects, but nobody was going to cry for a man who had lived a full life. And if you happened to see a guy with calves for sale, there was no reason not to do a little business while you were in town.

As I lay there, though, every voice startled me and made me struggle to keep the papers in place. The crowd probably saved me. If just one or two people had come along the sidewalk, they would have been peering into every car, especially strange ones. But that day there were neighbors to talk with and notice, and nobody glanced inside the white sedan.

Most of the voices faded after a time. I shifted position slightly and wondered when Doug and Cindy would ever come back.

Then there was a tap on the window above my feet. I didn't move. The tap came again, louder. "Hey, Larsy. Larsy." More tapping. "Larsy, you all right?"

It was Claude Hollinshead. There was no mistaking that wheezy, whining voice that people in the valley always tried to imitate. Everybody knew Claude, and everybody had a story about him. The easygoing people called him a character; the others called him a pest. He always showed up at somebody's house at five minutes before noon and then stood around and talked and didn't budge until he was asked to eat. (My mother tried to outlast him once. She held off dinner for over two hours before giving in and feeding him.)

"Larsy," Claude was calling, "you all right in there?"

There was nothing to do but raise myself up. The

papers went sliding down into the seat. "Yeah," I said, "I'm all right." I rolled down the window, glancing at the otherwise empty sidewalk.

"You're going to Notto's funeral, huh, Larsy?"

"Sure."

"Me too. I'll go in with you. He was a pretty good old guy, Notto. He was kinda ornery sometimes, though. You know what he did to me once? He filled up my soup with salt. So much salt I couldn't eat it. And then he said if I didn't like his cooking, I could go somewhere else and eat." Claude giggled. "It was a joke, see? I was surprised when they told me he died. You know, I'm older than him. And I always figured he'd be around when I was gone."

I was leaning back in the seat, trying to stay as hidden as possible. "You'll live to be a hundred, Claude."

He giggled again. "I might. Too mean to die." He looked in at me. "What were you doing on the floor there?"

I had been hoping that he wouldn't get to that question. "Hunting for something," I said. It was a weak answer, even for Claude.

"I looked in here, and I knew right away it was you. Nobody else got feet like you. What was it?"

"Huh?"

"What was you hunting for?"

I stared up at Claude's grinning face. He was dressed in a navy blue suit that was several sizes too big for him. The padded shoulders of the coat gave him the shape of a football player. I was staring at his necktie, which had pink flamingos on it, when I blurted out, "My necktie."

"Oh," he said, sounding puzzled. He seemed about to ask another question, but then he shook his head and said, "Sam Mauritsen told me that he heard you ran off. I stopped by your place yesterday and asked Old Hans, but he said it was none of my business. Your mother said you were gone on a little trip." He bent down and peered in at me. "Well?"

"What's that?" I was too busy looking around to pay much attention to Claude. Sooner or later somebody else would come along, and I would be all finished. What a laugh everybody would have. Lars Gustafson runs away from home and gets caught in Healdsburg—by Claude Hollinshead.

"Did you run off or what?"

"Nah, I just went on a little trip. I got back last night."

Claude giggled and pounded on the car. "Little trip, huh? And you didn't tell Old Hans you were going, huh? I'll bet he had a thing or two to say when you got back."

I started to answer that, but gave up and tried to smile.

"Where'd you go?"

"Huh?"

"On your trip. Where'd you go?"

"All over," I said.

Claude giggled again. "I'll bet Old Hans had a thing or two to say, all right. It's about time to go in, isn't it?" He reached into his pocket and took out a watch. "It's nine thirty right now. We're gonna be late if we don't hurry. You about ready?"

"I'll be along in just a minute. Don't wait for me."

"I don't mind," Claude said. "I'm not in a hurry."

"You go right on in," I told him. "I'll be there in a second."

"Hello, Archie," Claude called. Then he looked back at me. "I didn't figure Archie'd come to the funeral. He wouldn't even talk to Notto on the street. He was still mad about that time Notto's cow got loose and wrecked his garden."

"Go ahead and go with Archie," I said.

"He's inside by now. What are you waiting for, Larsy?"

Glancing around, I saw Cindy and Doug come out of the restaurant and head for the car. Germano Zipelli, whose farm was just south of ours, stopped and let them cross in front of his truck. "You go ahead and go inside, Claude," I said.

"Who're these people, Larsy?" Claude asked as Doug and Cindy climbed into the car.

"They're my cousins," I said. "They live in Willits." Cindy snorted.

"That's a good town," Claude told us. "My sister used to live in Willits."

Wilkins crossed the street and climbed into the car. "Let's get this show on the road," he shouted as he started the engine.

"I'll see you, Claude," I said.

"You're going to Notto's funeral, aren't you?"

"Sure, Claude. I just have to go get a necktie first."

"You don't need a necktie," Claude insisted. "Notto wouldn't care."

"See you later," I said, as the car pulled away.

"Who's your buddy in the zoot suit?" Wilkins asked.

"Some old bum," I said. "He thought I was somebody he knew, and then he was trying to get some money out of me." For some reason, I felt bad talking about Claude that way.

While I ate the doughnuts that Doug had brought me, I kept thinking about Claude. I wondered if he would tell people about seeing me. If he told them I had been right outside the funeral parlor hunting for a necktie, who would believe him? For Claude's sake, I hoped he didn't mention it.

As we crossed the bridge and left Healdsburg behind, I was feeling rotten and lonely. Seeing Uncle Charlie and the others got me remembering all the good times— making ice cream at the Farm Bureau picnic, eating popcorn at the movies with Uncle Charlie, having people stop and talk when I was working close to the road. I had known those people back there all my life, and now I was turning my back on them.

For a minute I wished I had had the courage to walk right into the mortuary and sit down beside my mother. I wasn't dressed for a funeral, but Claude was right— Notto wouldn't have cared.

9

For the next hour I tried to fight my way back to sleep, but my mind kept going back to Notto's funeral. Wilkins had located a radio station that came in without too much static. "I need a little noise to keep me awake," he shouted, apparently talking to either Doug or me. Wilkins seemed bored by the music, but he perked up whenever a commercial came on. "You hear that? Home cooking. What does that mean? It doesn't mean a thing. It sounds good to the suckers, though. Good old-fashioned home cooking? They probably get it out of a can." I grunted, figuring I was the only one awake. "You hear that one? Overstocked sale. What a joke! They buy a bunch of extra trash 'cause it's cheap and then have an overstocked sale."

I didn't always listen to what Wilkins was saying, but I gave him answers enough to keep him talking. The way I was feeling, anything was better than silence.

As we came over a hill south of the town of San Rafael, Wilkins stopped in the middle of a story about a car salesman and honked his horn. "Hey, kids, wake up!" he shouted. "Look out that way. You see that? That's your future home."

Cindy sat up and looked out. "I can't see anything."

Wilkins laughed and turned to look at Doug and me. "Don't you boys know what that is over there?"

Doug yawned and shook his head. "No," I said.

"That's San Quentin. You know about that, don't you? Biggest prison in the state."

We looked out toward the bay, trying to see which place he meant. I was never sure whether I actually spotted it.

"Yes, sir," Wilkins shouted over the music, "that's where you'll end up, likely as not. It's the American way. Today's punks turn out to be tomorrow's jailbirds." He looked back at us and laughed.

"What makes you so special?" Doug shouted back.

Wilkins kept smiling. "Oh, my, the boy is touchy."

"Don't give me that stuff," Doug shouted. "I don't have to put up with that kind of garbage from you. Who are you, anyway?"

Cindy turned around and glared. "Shut up, Douglas."

Wilkins turned down the radio and said, "I'd take it easy if I were you. I figure you got trouble enough without tangling with me." His voice was hard, but then he laughed and turned up the radio again.

Cindy shook her head at Doug, who mouthed something back at her. I didn't pay any attention. Off to our left was the blue water of the bay, and I was trying to catch a glimpse of the city.

For the next twenty minutes or so, nobody said anything. I stared out the window, trying to take in everything. A few times, as we came over a rise, I could see the skyline of San Francisco. In the meantime there was a lone sailboat in the bay and pockets of houses tucked up next to the hills.

Then we climbed the last long grade and passed through a tunnel to find the Golden Gate Bridge in front of us. "Look at that," Doug said, punching me on the shoulder. "I told you to stick with me."

Wilkins reached over and flipped off the radio. "See that little island out there? That's Alcatraz. Compared to Alcatraz, San Quentin is a Sunday school."

I stared at the island, remembering all the stories I had heard about convicts who tried to escape from there. The island was much closer to shore than I had pictured, and the main building looked a lot like my old junior high school.

"There's a whole lot to see right there," Wilkins said. "There's the bridge and the city and the prison. I'll pull over up ahead, and you can run across the highway and take a look. We're not in that much of a hurry."

"That's all right," Doug said.

"No trouble," Wilkins said. "Life's too short to pass up something like this." Just before we reached the bridge, he pulled the car onto the wide shoulder of the road. "Go ahead. You can get a great view of the whole works from right over there."

"I've seen it before," Cindy said as Doug and I were climbing out.

"Go ahead," Wilkins said. "Take five minutes and enjoy the view."

The three of us stood at the edge of the highway and waited for a break in the traffic. "Man, that bridge is something," I said.

Doug laughed. "I told you, Lars. That's just the beginning. There's a whole world waiting out there for us."

When we finally spotted an opening, we dashed across the road. Two buses and a few cars sat in the unpaved parking lot. At the end of the lot, people were standing behind a white metal railing and staring toward the water. We took our places along the railing just in time to watch a freighter pass beneath the bridge.

"That's the way to go," Doug said. "We ought to get jobs on a boat like that and go all over the world." He turned toward me and then looked past me. "That dirty rat!" he shouted. People around us turned and looked at him.

"What're you talking about?" I asked him.

"See for yourself," Doug said.

I looked across the highway and saw the empty shoulder where the sedan had been parked "I wonder what happened."

"Even *you* can figure it out," Cindy said. "The whole thing was a setup. He wanted to get rid of us, and he did it."

"What a rat!" Doug shouted, kicking a rock. People turned away from the bridge and looked at him.

"Oh, come off it," Cindy said. "What do you expect? You get smart with a guy that's giving you a ride—what do you think he's gonna do?" She turned back toward the water. "At least it's pretty here."

I looked at the bridge and the city beyond, but I was out of the mood for sightseeing. "Now what?" I asked.

"You see that city over there, Clodhopper?" Cindy said. "Douglas lost our ride for us, and nobody's going to stop and pick us up right at the bridge entrance. So you figure it out."

"No problem," Doug said. "After all the walking we've done, what's a little mile or two across the Golden Gate Bridge on a gorgeous day like this? Pretty as it is, I'd rather walk anyhow."

"Sure you would," Cindy muttered.

"Things are working out, Ace," Doug said to me. "I told you we'd be sleeping in Frisco tonight, and there it is." He waved his hand in the direction of the city. "Stick with the Tornado. I told you everything would be fine."

"You know what a tornado is?" Cindy said. "It's a whole bunch of wind."

As we moved along the walkway of the bridge, Doug talked about the people who had committed suicide there. After that I stopped a few times to stare at the water below. Whenever I looked straight down, my stomach would tighten and my hands would grab for the railing. I wondered how a person could get so unhappy with life that he would jump from there.

It was farther across the bridge than it looked, but I didn't really mind. The city was always there in front of me, and ships were moving in and out of the harbor. A tugboat passed directly beneath us, and the men on deck looked like ants.

I was so busy looking around that I kept lagging behind the others. When we were almost across the bridge, Doug suddenly stopped and leaned against the railing until I caught up to him. "Did you see him, Ace?"

"Who?"

"That cop."

"I didn't see anybody. I was looking out at the water."

"A cop just went past us, looking us over good. He went on through the tollbooths, but he may be waiting for us up ahead."

"Maybe we better turn around and go back," I said, my voice almost a squeak.

"Take it easy, man. We're okay. We'll go right along here until we get on the other side of the tollbooths. Then we'll cut across the highway and take the first road we can. He won't know what happened to us."

"Are you sure he was looking at us?" I asked, but Doug didn't even answer.

After that I didn't pay any attention to the scenery. I kept searching the area ahead of us, suspecting an ambush. The three of us walked along together, trying to look casual as we passed the toll plaza. The sight of all those men in uniforms bothered me, even though they were only leaning out of their little booths and collecting quarters.

There at the plaza the road must have been twelve lanes wide. A continual stream of cars moved in either direction. "We can't wait," Doug said, and dashed out into the highway. Cindy and I followed at his heels.

Drivers slammed on their brakes and hit their horns, even when they weren't that close to us. Somebody in a tollbooth began to yell at us, and the other toll takers joined in.

We couldn't do anything but keep running. We dashed across the final lanes of traffic and then headed right on the first road we saw. With all the commotion, I was sure the police wouldn't be far behind. We turned onto the first street we came to, then turned onto another narrow street before we slowed to a walk.

Once I was sure we weren't being followed, I began to wonder where we were. Instead of being in a city, we were in the middle of a parklike place. All around us were big eucalyptus trees and thick shrubbery. We followed the twisting road until we came to another twisting road, which led to another.

Every car that passed us was driven by somebody in a uniform. Most of the drivers looked us over, but nobody stopped. "Where are we, anyway?" I asked.

"Don't get excited, Ace," Doug said, but his voice was no steadier than mine. "This has to be Frisco. It's just some part I've never seen before. We'll be all right."

When we came to some buildings, we slipped around the edge of the parking lots, hoping that nobody would spot us. From the signs around there, we figured out that we were on an army base, but that didn't help us much. "We'll just keep going," Doug said. "Sooner or later we have to get out of here."

It wasn't much of a plan, but I had nothing better to offer.

We kept going and going. For a while we were in a cemetery, and later we were in the middle of a golf course. The worst part was that we didn't know whether we were breaking the law just by being there. We tried to hide whenever cars came by, and everywhere we turned we saw somebody in a uniform. Even though we knew these were soldiers, not policemen, we didn't dare get close to them.

Hours later we passed a grove of trees and saw the city in front of us. I was ready to get down and kiss the dirty sidewalk. We walked for several blocks, all uphill. The houses were different from any I had ever seen before—big three-story places with fancy shutters, but built right on the sidewalk and flush against other houses. "I wonder what it'd be like to live in a place like that," I said, but Doug and Cindy weren't listening.

After we had walked uphill for another block, I quit looking around me. "Do you know where we're going?" I asked Doug.

"Up the hill," he said.

"And when we get to the top," Cindy said, "we'll go down the other side. Now, do you have any more questions?"

"So we're lost, right?" I asked.

"Shut up for a while, Ace," Doug said. "We'll just keep going in a straight line. Sooner or later we'll hit a street we know."

There were only a few people on the sidewalk, most of them older men wearing overcoats and mufflers. They all seemed to be watching us, as if they knew we didn't belong there.

As we came closer to the top of the hill, Doug stopped and looked around. "I know one thing," he said. "I've never been here before. And I know something else. I know that if I don't rest for a while, I'm gonna die. I don't care what anybody thinks. I've got to sit down for a minute." He plopped down on the curb, with his feet sticking out into the street. Cindy and I joined him. A few cars drove by, and one or two old men walked past us, but nobody seemed to pay any attention.

We were still sitting on the curb when a taxi passed by and stopped in the next block. The driver came around to the sidewalk and helped a woman with her packages.

"Come on," I said. I ran up the hill toward the taxi, Cindy and Doug trailing along behind me. The driver came back across the sidewalk as I crossed the intersection. "Taxi!" I yelled.

He looked at me, waved his hand, and climbed into the car. I ran alongside as he started the engine and rolled down his window. "Where do you want to go?"

"I don't know. Just a second." I turned back to Doug and Cindy, who were walking by then. "Hey, where do we want to go?"

"Vanguard Hotel," Doug said, and gave the address. He opened the back door and climbed in. Cindy followed.

"You get in the back too," the driver told me. When the three of us were inside, he turned around. "All right, kids, let's see the money."

"We got money," Doug said.

"Suit yourself. I get paid now, or you don't go anywhere. I been burned too many times. Kids hop in, ride awhile, then jump out at a light and run off."

"Don't worry," I said. "We'll pay you."

"You bet you will, sonny. Either that, or you sit right here."

"Here." I handed him a five-dollar bill, and he smiled.

"Don't take it so hard, sonny. I'm just looking out for myself. The whole world's going crazy, and you gotta protect yourself."

"Vanguard Hotel," Doug said. "You got your money, so let's move it."

"Everybody's in a hurry," the driver moaned, putting the car into gear. "You're too young to be so impatient. You got your whole life to get things done."

The car leaped forward, throwing us back against the seat. At the first intersection the driver shifted into second gear as he roared past the stop sign. I sat with my mouth open. It was my first taxi ride, and my eyes kept moving back and forth from the streets to the clicking meter.

We drove through the center of the city, but I saw almost nothing. (Question: What was I looking at? Answer: The old man we almost hit, the delivery truck we almost hit, the car we almost hit . . .)

When the car skidded to a stop in the middle of a block, I looked forward to see what was in our path. Doug and Cindy climbed out quickly, and I scooted across the seat to the open door. "You owe me twenty cents more, sonny," the driver said, reaching back and clamping his hand on my wrist.

"The meter says four twenty."

"There's a charge of fifty cents for each extra passenger. So you owe me twenty cents more, plus a tip." I pulled another dollar out of my pocket, and he grabbed it. "Thanks, sonny. That's just right." He drove away as soon as I was out of the door.

"You gave him a tip after he cheated you?" Cindy asked. "I can't believe you."

"Leave me alone," I said. "Did you want me to make a big scene?"

"We're here," Doug said quickly. "That's the important thing. I don't care what that ride cost. It was worth it."

The lobby of the Vanguard Hotel stood between a laundry and a liquor store and was narrower than either of them. "We'll let Cindy go inside," Doug said. "The manager in there is this ape named Andy, and he doesn't like me much."

"Stay out of trouble," Cindy said as she went through the door.

Doug and I stood at the curb and watched the delivery trucks roar past. A steady stream of people walked past us—more old people and black people than I had ever seen.

When Cindy came back out of the hotel, her mouth was so tight that her lips hardly showed. "Oh, Douglas," she moaned, "Momma's not here anymore."

"What do you mean?" Doug asked.

"I went up and knocked on the door, and this old guy was living there. He'd never heard of Momma. So I came down and asked this new guy at the desk, and he says he's never heard of her either. I tried to get him to look back in his register to see when she left, but he says he's too busy. And he's sitting there working a stupid crossword puzzle."

"Now what?" I asked.

"If he's new, he doesn't know me," Doug said. "Give me a dollar, Lars." He grabbed the money and went inside.

Cindy and I stood by the window of the laundry. "Isn't this just dandy, Clodhopper? We walk till our feet are ready to fall off, and we sleep in the bushes, and then we finally get here and find out my mother doesn't even live here anymore. Things are really going our way, aren't they?"

"Well, we're in San Francisco, anyway. That's better than being in Willits."

"Terrific. Take a look around you. Isn't this a sweet little place? The Vanguard Hotel—how'd you like to come home to that at night? Doug and I lived here for four months. Take a look around here. This is real class. Pawnshops all around. Liquor stores. You ought to see this place at night. The decent people go inside and lock their doors, and the bums and the thugs come out."

I motioned toward a ragged old man who was wandering up the street toward us. "This one looks like he's out early."

"Great. That's all we need right now—a wino for company. This is Elroy coming. He hangs around here all the time. Somebody told me he lives in that alley down there."

"Howdy, there," Elroy said to me. His face was red and puffy, and his beard was several inches long—white, except for a brown stain on the right side.

"Hi," I said.

"Beat it, Elroy," Cindy said, looking away from him.

"I'm not talking to you. I'm talking to this boy here." He moved directly in front of me. "You gotta help me out. I'm starvin' to death."

"Get out of here, Elroy," Cindy said. "If you're hungry, all you have to do is go down to St. Anthony's or the Salvation Army."

Elroy laughed. "Don't like the food. Gives me indigestion." He turned away from us, purposely brushing against me. I held my breath, trying to escape the smell.

"You get the picture?" Cindy said. "Elroy, he's one of the good ones. He'll pester you, but that's all. The mean ones, they'll go after you. Oh, it's really fun around here. And you ought to see the slime that lives in the hotel."

"I'll bet." I watched Elroy move up to an old man on crutches, then walk on past, saying something over his shoulder.

"I had to clean rooms here. My mother had the job, but I did most of the work. You wouldn't believe some of the things I found. I had a piece of iron pipe that I carried in my belt, and I had a hatpin stuck in my hair. And I needed both of them, believe me. And Stupid in there can't stand Lytton Home just because they have rules."

Doug came out of the hotel shaking his head. "She left two weeks ago. The guy in there thinks she got fired. No forwarding address."

"Now what?" I asked.

"We could ask Mrs. Crawford," Cindy said. "I bet she'll know where Momma is." She turned to me. "Mrs. Crawford was the only person in this whole stinking place that was worth anything. She used to live in Tennessee, and she was always good to us."

"We'll let Lars go get her," Doug said.

"Why don't you do it? She doesn't even know me."

"Look, that jerk in there already told me to get lost. He took my buck and then said he'd call the cops if he saw me around again. But he's never seen you. Just go up there and tell her we're down here. She'll come down."

They told me exactly how to get to the elevator and how to find room 308, which belonged to Mrs. Crawford. "Don't even look toward the desk," Cindy said. "Just go right to the elevator like you owned the place."

The hotel lobby smelled of dead cigars and mildew and fly spray. A path had been worn in the flowered carpet from the front door to the elevator. I marched along that path and punched the button for the third floor.

"Stop right there, punk!" the desk clerk yelled.

I turned to face him and saw that he was pointing something at me, something covered by his newspaper. I figured it was more likely to be a finger than a gun, but I wasn't about to take a chance. "Sure," I said.

"Get away from that door and get out of here."

"I'm going to see Mrs. Crawford in room three-oh-eight," I said. The clerk snorted. "She's my aunt."

"Sure she is. And I'm Tarzan of the Apes."

"She's my aunt," I insisted, noticing that the paper was settling back onto the desk. "You can ask her."

"You got five minutes. You can go up there, but I want you out of this hotel in five minutes."

"Thank you, sir." He snorted again as I stepped into the elevator.

I located room 308 after one wrong turn, then pounded on the door until somebody across the hall threatened to kill me if I didn't stop. I headed back to the elevator, certain that Mrs. Crawford wasn't in her room.

As I stepped into the lobby, the clerk looked up at me. "Wasn't there, was she?"

"No, sir."

"She went out a couple of hours ago."

"Why didn't . . .?" I began before I caught myself.

"I figured a smart aleck like you could use the exercise. Now get out of here. If I see you around here again, I'll put the cops on you."

I headed for the door, and he picked up his paper. Cindy and Doug were waiting for me on the sidewalk. "She's not there," I said, then told them about the clerk.

"He's new," Doug said. "The other guys that worked here were always too lazy to bother about who was hanging around. We'll just wait him out. He probably goes off work pretty soon. When he's gone, we can try again."

"What'll we do in the meantime?" I asked.

Cindy groaned. "How about taking a walk? We haven't done that for a long time."

We killed an hour over hamburgers in a little hole-in-the-wall place, and we stopped somewhere else for a milk shake. In the meantime we walked, watching the rush hour traffic fill the streets. We sat on a bench in a small park until I fell asleep and Doug was sure that a motorcycle cop had his eye on us.

Finally we walked to Market Street and went to a movie theater called the Strand, which had cheap tickets and two westerns playing. I don't know how the movies were because I slept most of the time.

When we left the theater, we were hungry again. I wanted to find a grocery store and buy some bread and cheese, but Doug wouldn't hear of it. "You're in the city now, Lars. What do you figure the cops will think if they see us making sandwiches on the sidewalk in the middle of the night?" So we ended up at another hole-in-the-wall joint, eating another hamburger. (Question: How much catsup does it take to kill the taste of a really rotten hamburger? Answer: More than you can fit on a bun. I know because I tried.)

Afterward, we went back to the Vanguard Hotel. The sidewalks around there were much busier than before. People were sitting in doorways and standing in little clusters next to the buildings. Doug went into the hotel to see Mrs. Crawford while Cindy and I walked to the end of the block.

"Take a look around," she said. "You want to know what it's like to live in the city—here's your answer. The first week we lived here, there was a guy stabbed right across the street by those brown steps. The cops came and hauled him away, and that was it. I don't know if he died or not."

As we came to the corner, I saw three guys leaning against a car. They were a little older than we were, but they were the only other young people I had seen around there. "Hey, Cutie," one of them said to Cindy, "what's your name?" He was wearing a leather jacket with silver chains on the pockets.

Cindy and I turned back toward the hotel, trying not to seem in a hurry.

"Hey, Cutie, don't run away. Not when I need you so bad." The others laughed. I glanced over my shoulder, but they weren't following us.

"Neat place, huh, Clodhopper? This is good old San Francisco that you couldn't wait to get to."

"Look," I said, "I know it's crummy around here. But it's not my fault. You didn't have to come. You've been spending my money and treating me rotten ever since we started. So just lay off for a while, all right?"

"All right," she said quietly. I waited for her to go on, but she didn't say any more.

We stood beside the hotel door, where the light from the lobby lit up the sidewalk. After seeing the clowns on the corner, I wasn't anxious to do any more exploring. An old woman came up and asked us for a quarter. I shook my head and looked away from her. "Forget it, you stingy little snots," she grumbled.

When Doug stepped through the door, he looked at us and shrugged. "She's not there. The guy at the desk— this is a different one—doesn't know anything. I even asked that old duffer next door, that Mr. Bartell, but he didn't know much. He figured Mrs. Crawford would be back tomorrow for sure. He said if Mrs. Crawford is gone more than one night, she gets him to feed that dumb mynah bird of hers."

"Now what?" I asked.

"I don't know, Ace."

"I guess nobody'd rent us a hotel room, would they?" I asked.

"They might," Doug said. "But most likely they'd call the cops as soon as we got to our room."

"Oh, baby," I moaned.

"Come on, Champ. We'll go on back to Market Street. They've got a movie theater there that stays open all night. We'll be all right. A movie theater beats the heck out of lying in the bushes like we did last night."

"Let's go," I said. "I'm tired of standing here."

"Just a minute," Cindy said. "Maybe we'll get lucky. It's sure our turn. Clodhopper, do you remember those slots in back of the desk, where they have the keys and the mail?"

"I guess so."

"Go in there and ask the clerk something and see if there's a key in the slot for four-oh-one."

"What'll I ask him?"

"It doesn't matter. Ask him anything."

"Like what?"

"Anything. Come on. Move it, will you?"

I went into the lobby and marched straight to the desk. The clerk was watching a television set that was sitting on a shelf in the corner. I stood at the counter and looked down the row of pigeonholes until I found 401. There was a key sitting in the box.

"You want something?" the clerk said without turning around.

"Do you know what time it is?" I asked, already headed for the door.

"About a quarter to ten," he said. "This program's about half over."

Cindy and Doug were out of sight when I stepped onto the sidewalk. I stood beside the door and looked in both directions, feeling helpless and alone.

Doug stepped out of a doorway and called, "Hey, Ace. Over here."

"I didn't know where you were."

"Cops drove by, and we didn't want to advertise. Was the key there?"

"Yeah, it was there."

"I'll see you in a minute, then," Cindy said, walking back toward the hotel.

"What's going on?" I asked.

"This way, Lars." Doug started in the opposite direction. "She'll go inside and let us in the emergency exit. It's clear around the back." He and I walked down a narrow alley, past a huge pile of cardboard boxes. I hurried to keep as close to Doug as I could.

As we passed a row of garbage cans, something moved behind them. "What was that?" I whispered.

"Who knows? Cat maybe. Or a rat."

I hurried on, forcing myself not to look back.

Ahead of us a door swung open, and light poured into the alley. Cindy stepped into the light and waved for us to hurry. As we dashed into the building, she pulled the door closed. We were in a narrow hallway, lit by a single bare bulb.

"Keep it quiet," she whispered in my ear. "We'll go down the hall about halfway. There's a stairwell there." I followed her past a dozen brown doors, through a metal door, and up a flight of narrow stairs. The walls on each side of the stairs were covered with filthy words and pictures. At the first landing we went through another metal door to another hallway and the same kind of brown doors. "We can take the elevator now. It's only two flights up, but those stairs give me the creeps."

The fourth-floor hallway had been painted white some time before, but the paint had been put over flowered wallpaper. In the spots where the paint was chipping, you could see the old paper.

"Down that way's four-sixteen," Cindy whispered. "Our old place. This room up here—four-oh-one—has a lock that doesn't work. I used to have to clean it, so I know. It's a crummy room, but it beats walking the street all night."

I was relieved when we were safely inside 401, even when I saw what the place looked like. The walls were yellowish white, except for the spots where the old wallpaper showed through. The only furniture was a straight-backed wooden chair, a small table that had once been painted yellow, and a bed with two blankets. I opened the only other door, which led to a closet, empty except for a single wire hanger.

"The bathroom's down the hall," Cindy said, "but you're gonna have to run fast to beat me to it. I don't care if I don't have a towel. I need a bath."

While she was gone, Doug and I pulled the mattress off the bed and put it on the floor. "Cindy can have the box springs," he said. "They look better than this mattress anyway."

Later that night I lay on that lumpy mattress and tried

to push the thoughts of home out of my mind. (Question: How well did that work? Answer: About as well as the rest of our plans did.)

The mattress smelled so ferociously of cigarettes that I had to lie on my back to escape the stench. All around me were the strange noises of the city—car horns, the hiss of truck brakes, muffled voices, a siren somewhere far off. As I lay there and listened, I decided that the worst thing about running away was the sleeping arrangements.

10

We slept far into the morning. Several times I opened my eyes, thought about getting up, then rolled over and drifted off again.

Above my head, the lock on the door rattled and clicked. My eyes snapped open, and I looked up to see a dark-haired woman standing in the doorway. "What you doing here?" she asked.

I started to answer, but she shut the door before I could think of anything. I could hear her feet padding down the hall.

"Doug!" I shouted, shaking his shoulder. "Doug!"

He sat up quickly, throwing the blanket to one side. "What's the matter?"

"Somebody just came in here."

He settled back a little. "You sure? Or are you dreaming?"

"A woman came in, asked what we were doing here, and then took off."

"Cindy!" Doug shouted. "Hey, Cindy!"

Cindy rolled over and faced us. Her hair was strung across her face, and her eyes were almost shut. "Huh?"

"We'd better get up and get out of here," Doug told her. "Somebody came in here and spotted us."

Cindy threw her legs over the side of the bed and pulled her skirt down over her knees. "Who?"

"A woman with black hair," I said, trying to picture her again. "About forty or so. She opened the door and asked what we were doing here."

"Let's go," Cindy said, reaching for her shoes. "It must have been one of the maids."

We pulled on our shoes and stuffed our pockets with the things we had taken out. Doug opened the door a few inches and whispered, "It's too late. Just stay by me."

We moved into the hallway just as the woman I had seen was approaching the door. Beside her was a heavy-set man carrying a sawed-off baseball bat. "Them's the ones," the woman said. She turned and headed in the opposite direction.

"Hello, Andy," Doug called out.

The heavyset man moved into the center of the hall-way. "I had trouble with you before," he said, pointing his bat at Doug. "I had trouble with you, and I had trouble with your mother."

Cindy stepped between Doug and the bat. "But you never had any trouble with me, did you, Andy?"

He shrugged. "I guess not."

"We were in a bad way last night," Cindy said. "We had to see Mrs. Crawford down in three-oh-eight, and she wasn't there. We didn't have any place to stay, and it was really late. I remembered that the door on four-oh-one wouldn't lock, so we came up here to sleep."

"You got no business around here," Andy said. "I fired your mother awhile back, and I don't want anything to do with any of you."

"Do you know where my mother went?" Cindy asked quickly. "We're trying to locate her."

"I don't know, and I don't care. I don't want nothing to do with her. And anybody that sleeps in this hotel pays for the room."

I started toward my pocket, but Cindy was faster. "Come on, Andy. If we had any money, do you think we'd be sleeping with the bugs up here in four-oh-one?"

"Listen, sister, if there's any bugs in there, you brought 'em with you. Now you clear out of here, and don't ever come back. If I see you around here again, you'll wish I hadn't."

"We're gone," Cindy said, walking past him.

As I tried to step around him, Andy shoved the bat into my stomach. "You hear me, Skinny? You understand what I said?"

"Yes, sir."

"You clear out, and don't ever come back." He pushed the bat farther into my stomach. I moved backward until I was pressed against the wall. "I'm not a guy you want to fool with." He prodded me once, then pulled back the bat.

"Yes, sir," I said, and headed away.

He reached out with the bat and rapped my shoulder. It looked like a little tap—the kind of motion you'd use to swat a fly—but the pain almost knocked me down. I clenched my teeth and managed to keep moving. "Maybe that'll help you remember," he said.

As soon as I was past Andy, Doug turned and ran the other way. Andy took a few steps after him, then stopped as Doug went through the door to the stairs. "Hurry up, Lars," Cindy shouted, holding the elevator door. Andy rushed toward us until the door began to close. Then he stopped and swore at us until the door clicked shut.

Doug was waiting for us in front of the hotel. "You all right, Ace?"

I moved my arm up and down. "It only hurts when I laugh."

"Let's move," Cindy said. "There's no telling what he might do."

We walked a few blocks to a restaurant, where we discovered that it was too late to get breakfast. After ordering hamburgers and milk, we sat back and looked at each other.

"I don't know," Cindy said. "I hope I don't look as bad as you two."

"You don't," I told her. "You look worse."

That was enough to send her off to the rest room. I stayed at our table while Doug went to clean up. While they were gone, I counted my money and was amazed to find that I had only eleven dollars left.

As we sat over our empty plates, I rubbed my shoulder. "Look, we have to do something. We're running out of money, and we don't have any place to stay."

"It's all right," Doug said. "We'll be okay. Tonight we'll go back and see Mrs. Crawford and find out where Momma is staying. Then we'll get our clothes washed and get some money and head out." He looked at Cindy. "And she'll be staying with Momma."

"You bet your life I will," Cindy said. "If you think I want any more of this runaway business, you're out of your mind."

"Now what?" I asked. "What do we do all day? Walk around some more?"

"Hey, don't start sounding that way. Things are gonna be all right."

"Sure they are," I said. "Everything's just great."

He leaned over and punched me. "Come on, Lars. You start in that way, and I don't know what I'll do. It's bad enough with Cindy always moaning. I can't take two of you. Things are gonna work out."

"Hey, Clodhopper," Cindy said, "you got the feeling you heard all this before?"

"You two better watch what you say," Doug told us, starting to grin. "If you don't, you're gonna feel pretty stupid. Just wait till you find out what I got planned for us this afternoon."

"I'll bet I can guess," I said. "We're gonna take a walk."

Cindy laughed, but Doug just pointed his finger at me. "Just for that, I'm not gonna tell you. You'll have to wait and see." He laughed and punched me again. "I gotta teach you to quit being a big fudd."

"A fudd? What's that?"

"A fudd is somebody that sits around and complains when he should be out having a good time. You want to come along, or do you want to sit here like a fudd?"

I stood up and headed for the door. "Let's go."

"I'm still not gonna tell you what the surprise is. You'll just have to wait and see."

We walked a long way, but I didn't complain anymore. Doug had whispered something to Cindy, and she had been grinning ever since. "This walk is the only bad part, Ace," he said. "But it's worth a little walk. You just wait and see. We're gonna catch a streetcar up here. There's probably a closer place to catch it, but this is the only one I'm sure about."

"Don't worry about me," I said. "I'm better now. I'm all through being a fudd." I *did* feel a little better. After all, I was about to take my first ride on a streetcar.

The streetcar was a noisy contraption, with a cow-catcher on the front and an open-air platform at the back. Cindy went inside the car and found a seat, but I stayed on the platform where I could get a better view. The jerky, rattling ride reminded me of the boxcar, but I held on to a metal pole and tried to take in everything around me.

The platform slowly filled with people, and several hands grasped my pole. Doug squeezed between two men and spoke in my ear. "Look out ahead of us, Lars. That's the ocean right out there."

"Oh, man," I blurted out, "is that where we're going?" I realized then that people were looking at me.

Doug laughed and spoke out too. "We're gonna walk barefooted in the sand and let those waves crawl over our toes. You wait." He laughed again, and several people around us smiled.

"That water's a little cold," a man said.

"The colder the better," Doug said. "I love cold water."

"Then you're going to be happy as a clam," the man told him.

Doug pushed up next to me and muttered, "You know what, Ace? The ocean isn't even the surprise." He laughed and stepped back.

As the streetcar rattled to a stop the conductor shouted, "End of the line." I followed the others off the platform and waited for Doug on the sidewalk.

"You know what this is?" he shouted. "You know where you are? This is Playland. What do you think about that?"

I just stood and stared. It was like all the carnivals I had ever seen, gathered together in one spot. Never in my life had I seen anything so spectacular. "Oh, man," I said. "Oooh, man." I took a few steps back so that I could get a clear view of the whole place.

Doug grabbed my arm. "Come on, Lars. Let's go take a look."

We walked from one end of the midway to the other, drifting along with the crowd. We stopped now and then to watch a sailor throw baseballs or a little boy who wanted to get off the merry-go-round in the middle of the ride. Doug was disappointed that the roller coaster was closed. "I tell you, man, it was fun to stand here and watch the people come off that thing. Some of them were so scared, their faces were snow white."

I didn't care about the roller coaster. There was already too much for me to take in. There was Laughing

Sal, the enormous clown figure outside the Fun House, shaking her sides and moving her huge lips as the laugh track echoed over and over. There were the rides— Shoot the Chutes, Tilt-a-Whirl, Octopus—and the people screaming as they were tossed around. There were the games and the barkers shouting "A prize every time" or "Win one for your girl friend, soldier" or "It's an easy game—all it takes is a little luck and a quarter." And the food—candied apples, snow cones, cotton candy, foot-long hot dogs.

We drifted back the way we had come, stopping more often to watch the rides and the games. We stood for a long time behind the rope barrier and watched the action of the Dodger Cars—saucerlike contraptions with rubber bumpers all the way around them. There were continual crashes, and nobody ever dodged.

When Cindy suggested that we go to the ocean for a while, I was happy to follow along. I had seen so much that I needed some time to sort it all out. We crossed the wide parking lot and the highway, then trotted down the cement steps to the beach. Leaving our shoes and socks on the bottom step, we trotted through the sand to the freezing water. Doug and I rolled up our pantslegs and dashed through the surf. At first Cindy hung back, but soon she was running along with us.

Twenty minutes later we were perched on the seawall, brushing the sand from our feet and trying to rub some life back into our toes. I pulled on my shoes quickly, eager to get back to Playland.

"Hurry it up," I told them. "Maybe this is old stuff to you two, but I've never been to Playland before."

"We're real old-timers," Cindy said. "Doug and I came here once last year. Daddy brought us here the first weekend we were in San Francisco."

Doug stood up and danced around. "I still got sand stuck between my toes. I can feel it ooching around down there." He looked across the parking lot. "You know what? Some day I'm gonna come here with a hundred dollars, and I'm gonna ride on everything I want to and play all the games. If I want to throw baseballs, I'll throw 'em till my arm hurts. I'll bring somebody along just to carry all the teddy bears I win."

I leaned back against the wall and laughed. "You bring the hundred, and I'll carry your teddy bears for you."

"I just wish the roller coaster was running. You ought to see it come roaring down that back part there."

"Did you ride it when you were here?"

"Nah, Ace, we didn't have any money. We'd just got to town, and my father hadn't been paid yet. We just took the streetcar out to the beach and walked through, the way we're doing today."

"You gonna talk or go to Playland?" Cindy shouted as she dashed across the highway.

We wandered through the midway again, stopping for a while to watch the Ski-Ball players. "I could have a hundred bucks," Doug said, "and I wouldn't spend a dime on that dumb game. All you get if you win is a stupid ticket, and it takes about a hundred tickets to get anything decent."

Soon we were back by the Dodger Cars again. Each time the power was shut off and the cars came to a stop,

I looked over at Doug and Cindy, wondering if they wanted to drive those cars as badly as I did. I knew that it would be crazy to throw away what little money we had on something like rides, but I wanted to try those Dodger Cars just the same.

Finally Doug turned to me and asked, "Hey, Lars, how much bread we got?"

I knew what he was really asking, but I hadn't quite made up my mind. "Not much. About eight bucks or so."

"What do you think? You think maybe we ought to try those things one time?"

I looked down at my hands. "I don't know. It doesn't make sense to—" I stopped suddenly, realizing how much I was sounding like my father. I turned to Doug and smiled. "Why not?"

"I can't think of a reason, Ace."

"If you're gonna do it," Cindy said, "then I want to do it too."

We trotted to the window, bought tickets, and climbed into our cars. When the power was turned on, I pushed the pedal as far down as it would go and raced madly around the floor. At first Doug and I carried on our own private battle. We would crash together, spin, maneuver for position, and crash again. Then we ganged up on strangers, laughing and shouting as we attacked from both sides. Cindy joined us for a minute, then hit Doug and sent his car spinning up against the wall. That started another private battle. When the ride was over and the attendant cleared the floor, we dashed to the ticket booth so that we wouldn't miss a turn.

Even in the middle of the excitement, I never forgot about our situation. I knew that what we were doing was crazy, and I loved every minute of it. After three rides on the cars we raced down the midway to Shoot the Chutes. From there we went to Laff in the Dark, a spookhouse that scared me more than I let on. Then there was the Fun House, where we wandered through the mirrors and slid down long polished slides, giggling and carrying on like eight-year-olds.

When we left the Fun House, we bought foot-long hot dogs and carried them across the parking lot to the sea-wall. We sat there in the mist and watched the sun go down behind a bank of fog. For that moment I was completely satisfied. I could have died right then without any regrets.

11

As night came on the wind picked up strength and began swirling sand around our feet. Cindy stood up and looked back at the ocean for a long minute. "We'd better go, I guess."

"I hate to leave," I said, getting up slowly.

"Hey, Lars," Doug said, "how much money we got left?"

For just a minute as I reached into my pocket, I could feel my mood begin to slip away. "Not as much as I had before." I pulled a handful of change from my pocket and dumped it on the seawall in front of me.

"How much you got there, Ace?"

Looking down at the pitiful pile of nickels and dimes, I couldn't stand to count it. The whole thought of money depressed me. "You figure it out." I shoved the coins in front of Doug, who began sorting them into neat stacks.

I turned away and watched the ocean, trying to recapture the peaceful feeling that I had had before.

"Beautiful!" Doug shouted. "We got it made in the shade. We got our streetcar fare, and we got enough to ride the Dodger Cars one more time. And you'll still have twenty-one cents left over."

It was insane to think of blowing our money on one last ride, but at that moment it sounded like the most marvelous idea I had ever heard. We ran across the parking lot, screaming with laughter. We stood in line, bought our tickets, and raced to get what we figured were the fastest cars. I kept laughing through all the bumps and spins, wishing the ride would never end.

But the ride did end. We cleared the floor and walked slowly back to the streetcar stop. When the next car arrived with its load of excited passengers, I was jealous for just a minute. Then I boarded the empty car, took a seat beside the window, and grinned while the city slid past. When we reached our stop, I was still staring out the window. Doug tapped me on the shoulder and said, "Let's go, Champ." It took me a minute to realize where I was.

When we reached the Vanguard Hotel, Cindy volunteered to go inside. "That clerk never even saw me last night. I'll just scoot right over to the elevator."

I rubbed my sore shoulder. "Watch out for Andy."

Doug and I waited by the alley entrance, where it was a little darker. People drifted past, but nobody seemed to see us. I wondered if we were beginning to fit in with the other street people.

While I stood there, I tried to hold on to the magic of the day by thinking back to moments at Playland—that hot dog, that eerie spookhouse, the time I spun the sailor all the way around in the Dodger Cars, the crazy mirrors. Soon I was grinning again.

Thinking about the day, I found it hard to believe that I had spent all my money that way. It seemed as if I should be sorry for doing such a crazy thing, but I wasn't sorry at all.

Cindy was crying when she came back out of the hotel. She reached into her purse for a Kleenex and wiped her eyes before she said anything. "That slimy old bag. I thought she was our friend. You remember what she used to tell us, Douglas? She used to say that having other people from Tennessee around was like having a family again. Well, that old bat just made herself an orphan."

"Where's Momma?" Doug asked.

Cindy started to say something, then shook her head. "Oh, Douglas," she moaned. He gave her a little push. "Douglas, she doesn't know where Momma went. She said Momma went with some guy named Roy to some town called Turlock. Momma told her they were tired of the city, and they were going to some place out in the country, where this Roy had some kinfolks."

"Don't tell me," Doug groaned.

"Momma's gone," Cindy said. "She's just gone."

Doug took several noisy breaths and blew out the air slowly. "Oh, man, we're up against it. We better talk to Mrs. Crawford. Maybe she can—"

"Forget it," Cindy said. "That old bag. She was all honey and biscuits when I came in, and then when I told her we were in trouble and needed a place to stay, it was a different story. I told her we didn't mind sleeping on the floor, and I said we'd be gone first thing in the morning. But she wouldn't have it. All of a sudden she started saying what a sick woman Momma is, how her mind is going. And she said that we shouldn't be out like we are."

"You shoulda told her . . ." Doug muttered.

"I kept holding back, trying to get her to let us stay. Finally she said I better go, that she had to get some sleep. I couldn't stand it. I just went crazy and called her every name I could think of. And what good did that do? It didn't even make me feel better."

"I oughta go up there and tell her a thing or two," Doug said. "I'll bet I could come up with a few names you never even thought of. Who's she think she is? Remember all those times we went and got groceries for her and cleaned out that dumb bird cage? I'd give her something to think about."

"Forget it," Cindy said. "She'd just call Andy, and we'd be in more trouble."

We stood in the shadows for a long time. (Question: Where do you go in San Francisco on a Saturday night when you have twenty-one cents to your name? Answer: Nowhere at all. You just keep standing in one spot and trying to think.)

Cindy stepped back from the wall and gave me a shove. "I keep waiting for you to say 'Now what?' "

"I didn't say a word, did I?"

Doug took a long breath and blew it out in a loud sigh. "All right," he began. "Things are a little tough right now, but we'll be okay. We've had some tough breaks—more than our share. But things'll even up. We'll be okay."

"Sure we will," Cindy said.

"Look," Doug said, "we're okay. We're in San Francisco at least, not Lytton. We're gonna be all right."

"I'd rather be in Lytton," Cindy said.

"Well, we don't have that choice, do we? Just lay off, will ya? You always kick me when I'm down."

"That's because you need kicking," Cindy said. "We're not okay, and you know it. We're out of money, and we have nothing to eat and no place to stay. Except for that, we're okay."

"We'll make it," Doug insisted. "We can't do it all at once. Right now we need a place to sleep. That's number one. I'd go back up to four-oh-one, but I'll bet Andy's watching it. He'll probably get out of bed in the middle of the night just to go up there and check."

"Forget that one," I said. "My shoulder still hurts."

Doug began to move around, dancing from one foot to the other. "Maybe I could sweet-talk Mrs. Crawford into letting us stay there. I could say that I just came up to apologize for you, that you were ashamed of the way you acted. Maybe I could get her to change her mind. She always liked me."

"Forget it," Cindy said. "I wouldn't give her the satisfaction even if it would work, and it won't. You know what that old bag said about you? She said she bet that worthless, good-for-nothing brother of mine got me into this. So you can go up there and do all the sweet-talking you want to. See where it gets you."

"All we need is just a place for one stinking night," Doug said. "Right now I'd settle for that barn outside of Healdsburg. Anywhere at all."

"I was thinking," I said. "Maybe we could sell my

watch and get enough money for that all-night movie theater you were talking about."

"Who's gonna buy it?" Cindy said.

"Wait a minute," Doug shouted. "Ace, you just reminded me of something." He let out a laugh. "We got it made. Cindy, do you remember that old movie theater that Grady showed us?"

"That place?"

"Sure. It's not that far from here. It'll be great. For tonight, at least."

"If the rats don't eat our toes."

"There's this old movie theater," Doug told me. "It's down this way a few blocks. This old guy that used to work there took us inside one time. I just hope they haven't torn it down already. If they haven't, it's empty and just waiting for us."

"It's not empty," Cindy said. "It's full of bugs and rats."

"How do we get inside?" I asked.

"No problem. There's this side door that's busted. You know, one of those emergency exits. We went in that way with Grady."

"Yeah," Cindy said. "I only went inside about three feet. It's awful in there."

"Look," Doug told her, "if you've got a better idea, let's hear it."

"I don't have any ideas at all," she said quietly.

"Then you just better hope that the old place hasn't been torn down, because I don't have a second choice."

The Rex Theater was still standing, a big stucco building with yellow paint peeling off the front. Except for the boards nailed across the entrance, the theater didn't look much worse than the other old buildings in that block.

We headed down a dark alley and tugged open the broken door. I had been expecting a theater—with seats and a screen—but the inside of the building had been stripped. Except for the slant of the floor and the raised stage, you couldn't have told it ever had been a theater. We had no flashlight, of course, but Doug kept lighting matches as we made our way forward through piles of broken plaster and splintered boards. He finally located some cardboard and made a torch, which lasted for a minute or two.

After some stumbling around, we located a section of the narrow stage that was flat and not too cluttered. While Cindy held another torch, Doug and I cleared away boards and chunks of plaster until there was room for us to lie down. Then Doug rounded up a few musty newspapers and cartons, which we used to smooth out our sleeping area.

Doug made another trip to the alley and came back with a pile of newspapers. "Next best thing to blankets," he said.

We lay down and wrapped newspapers around our-selves. The whole thing struck me funny. "I can't believe this. The only place I ever saw people sleeping in news-papers was in the comic books."

"It's okay, Ace," Doug said. "Just hang on awhile. Things will get better."

"I can do without the pep talk," Cindy muttered.

"I'm not complaining," I said. "That Playland—that

was something. Those Dodger Cars—I never rode on anything like them before." Nobody answered me. I grinned into the darkness as I lay there on my cardboard mattress. I was cold and uncomfortable, of course, but that seemed to be par for the course.

12

When I awoke the next morning, sunshine was streaming through a big hole in the center of the ceiling. Around that hole the ceiling sagged, and broken boards stuck out at odd angles. The whole section looked as if it might come crashing down any minute.

"Hey, Champ," Doug said to me, "how you doing?" He was crouched in a corner, kneeling next to a cardboard box.

"I'm all right," I said. "What're you doing over there?"

"Shaving."

"What for? You don't have enough whiskers to bother with."

"I've got more than you."

"That's not saying anything."

"I got just enough to look stupid after a couple of days." He made a few passes along his chin. "It'd work better if I had some water, but I'm doing all right. It doesn't have to be too good. I just don't want to look like a scrounge."

"What do you have in mind?"

"I'm gonna find us some breakfast. You just wait here. I'll be back with the goodies before Cindy wakes up."

"Where are you going?"

"Leave it to me, Champ. I've been doing this whole thing wrong. All this time I've been trying to find my old lady so she could help us out. That kind of stuff is crazy, and we know it. You want something in this world, you have to get it for yourself. From now on, we don't depend on anybody. You wait. We'll make it. We'll get the Boll Weevil Express back on track and be in Idaho before you know it, pulling fish out of the river like nobody's business." He straightened his shirt and combed his hair carefully. "See you in a little while." He went out the broken door and pushed it closed behind him.

"Hey, Clodhopper," Cindy said as soon as he was gone, "come here."

I scooted over to where she was lying, still wrapped in newspapers. "Doug'll be back in a little while."

"I know. I heard all that." She sat up and shoved the newspapers to one side. Her face was a little puffy, but when you figured where she had slept, she still looked fresher and prettier than she had any right to. "Look, we need to talk. This whole thing is dumb. How much has Douglas told you about Daddy?"

"Not too much." I hunched into a ball, wrapping my arms around my knees. "It's cold in here."

"Do you know when we last heard from him? Did Douglas tell you that?"

"No."

"It's been most of a year. Right after he left us, maybe a week or two later, he sent us a postcard from some little town in Idaho—Twin Falls, I guess. And that's all we know. He never even sent an address. He just said he'd found the right place for himself and for us to come visit him sometime."

"Well, I guess this is the time."

Cindy snorted. "You're really dumb, you know that? Look, every town he came to, he was sure it was the right town for him, and he never stayed more than a month or two in any of 'em. Are you starting to get the picture?"

"Okay," I said. "So he might not be there. If you figure we can't find him, then maybe you should go back to Lytton."

She threw a piece of cardboard at me, hitting me in the shoulder. "You'd like that fine, wouldn't you?" she shouted. "Just have me go off and leave you two alone. She reached behind her, and I moved back a little, not sure what she might find to throw.

"Don't go getting mad at me," I said. "What did I do? You're the one saying he isn't there."

"All right," she said, her voice still angry. She settled back and pulled some of the newspapers around her. "Look, you want to hear the whole sad story? I mean it. This is the real thing. No games. No smart cracks. You want to hear it?"

"If you want to tell it," I said.

"Douglas and I grew up in a little town in Tennessee. Lived there all our lives. Daddy worked in a mine, and

Momma worked some at a diner that belonged to her cousin. Then when I was about ten or so, there was a cave-in, and Daddy got trapped. They got him out the next day, and he wasn't hurt bad or anything, but he was never the same after that. He started talking about how terrible it was to work in a mine and about all the things he wanted to do before he died. Then one night he came home from the mine and said we were moving. My mother fought and argued with him. She'd lived her whole life in that town. But he said he was going, and she could either come or not. So we all went." Cindy reached out and pulled some more newspapers around her legs. "Douglas and I, we didn't know what to think. We'd never been much of anywhere. Just dumb little kids that had lived in the same place all our lives. Sort of like you."

"Come on," I said.

"Well, then, all we did in the next couple of years was move. We kept settling in and then moving again. Daddy would get a job, and he'd love it, and then three days later he'd cuss out the boss and get fired. And off we'd go again. It was like he wasn't himself anymore. At nights, sometimes, he'd get crazy and say all kinds of awful things to us. Then the next day he'd cry and say he was sorry and promise never to do it again. But he always would."

"Oh, man," I said, not knowing what else to say. Never in my life had anybody talked to me the way she was talking—telling things that people usually kept secret. I wanted to say something to her that would help, but I couldn't think of anything at all.

"Then last summer he took off and left us, and all we've heard since then was that one postcard. There's no telling where he is by now. I don't particularly want to find him. Neither does Douglas, but he thinks he does. Or part of him does." She reached her hand toward me, and some of the newspapers slid away. "Does that make any sense?"

"Some, I guess." I leaned forward and tucked the newspapers around her.

"Thank you," she said quietly. "You see, Douglas knows what Daddy's like now. He knows that Daddy is never gonna be the way he used to be when we were kids. But Douglas gets these goofy ideas that he talks himself into believing. Just like coming here to San Francisco to get money from Momma. That was crazy, and he knew it. Momma hasn't had two dollars back to back since Daddy left us. Where was she supposed to come up with enough for bus tickets?"

"Good question."

"You gotta see what Douglas is really like. He gets caught up in these stupid dreams, and he won't face facts. Look, Momma's had a tough time ever since we left Tennessee, and she's been worse since Daddy left. When Douglas got hooked up with this Mallory guy and was out stealing car parts all night, Momma didn't even seem to notice. He did tell you about Mallory, didn't he?"

"He said he got caught stealing car parts."

"That was just as dumb as the other things, but save that for now. When he got caught and the social worker came around, Momma just said she couldn't handle him anymore. The social worker took a good look around and then talked Momma into sending us to Lytton. That way, Douglas and I wouldn't be separated, anyway. Momma cried and promised to write us every week, and she said she'd get a place and have us back with her as soon as she could. How many letters do you think we got?"

"Not many, I guess."

"Two. And the second one was a valentine. You see what I'm talking about? Douglas came down here to get money from Momma, and he knew better. But he came all the same."

"Yeah, I see what you mean."

"And he knows better than this running away, too. You know what's gonna happen, don't you? He's already been in trouble, and he's been a stinker at the home the last few weeks. If he gets picked up now, the Lytton people probably won't take him back. That means he'll wind up in Preston. You know what Preston is? It's reform school. It's bars on the windows and solitary confinement if you don't behave. So that's what you gotta understand. All this stupid dreaming is about to send Douglas off to prison."

I looked at Cindy and shook my head. "But what do you want from me? Maybe we never should have run off, but we did. We can't change that."

"Douglas has one chance," she said quietly. "If he would call Major Binkley and ask to come back, things might work out. But if we keep going until we're caught, Douglas will have his ticket to Preston."

"But there's no way he'd make a call like that."

"Not while you're here." She leaned toward me, her eyes on mine. "Look, he's your friend, isn't he?"

"Of course he is."

"Then you've got to help your friend. You've got to help him because he's not strong enough to do it on his own."

"I don't get it," I said. "What do you want me to do?"

Cindy reached out and took my hand. "I want you to go. Will you do that?"

"Go where?"

"Anywhere you want. Just away from here."

"What good would that do?"

"If you weren't here, he'd think about going back. Can't you see that? He'll never give up while you're here."

I sat and looked at her, feeling her hand on mine. "You want me to go off and leave you?"

"It's the only way. Otherwise, you're sending your friend to reform school."

I don't know what I would have done if we had been left alone for a few more minutes. Before I could answer, though, the side door creaked open, and I yanked back my hand.

"It's time for breakfast," Doug yelled. He stepped inside quickly, pulling the door closed behind him. "Man, it's dark in here after being out in the sun. What do you want, powdered sugar doughnuts or chocolate ones?" He came toward the stage, pulling packages out from beneath his coat.

"Chocolate," I said.

"You can still take off," Cindy whispered. "After we eat, you can head for a service station and just not come back."

"Here you go," Doug shouted, tossing me a cellophane package. "All I got for us to drink is some pineapple juice. The dairy case was right by the cash register, so I couldn't get us any milk."

"No complaints," I said, tearing open my package and biting into a doughnut.

I was too busy with my food to be concerned with anything else. The first time I realized that something was wrong was when Doug suddenly waved his arms and then held his finger to his lips.

"This here's the door," a boy's voice was shouting. "I seen him go right in here."

"You guys get around the other side," a much deeper voice shouted.

"Quick!" Doug whispered. "We gotta hide."

The three of us hurried in the same direction—away from the door. There was a mound of old boards and plaster in the far corner of the stage. Because there was nowhere else to go, all three of us crouched behind that pile and waited.

"I seen him," the boy's voice said again. "He come right down the alley and through this door."

"Give me a hand with this thing," a third voice said. He swore as the door creaked open. "It's sure dusty inside here. I don't know why somebody doesn't tear down a place like this."

There was a lot of coughing and some more swearing as they clumped inside the place.

"Hey, you," somebody shouted. "Come on out. You can't get away."

"He's got to be in here somewhere," one of them said. "We need to stick together, though. Let's wait a minute till our eyes get used to the dark."

"I might smother first. You talk about dusty—this is the real stuff."

"Look at that hole in the roof. Looks like something fell on it."

I knelt behind the mound and tried to think. There was no way to get out, and our hiding place was pitifully obvious. Cindy was pushed up against me, and I could feel her body trembling.

"Maybe he went out the front," one of them said.

"Couldn't do it. It's all boarded up. He's in here, all right."

"You might as well give up," somebody shouted.

"Just stay together," somebody else said. "We'll find him."

I could hear their feet crunching on the broken plaster as they began to move through the theater. "You know, this old place was really something when I was a kid."

"Shoot, Morris, I didn't think they had movies when you were a kid."

"He's got to be up in the front. There's nowhere else for him to be."

Next to me, I could feel Cindy's body move in little short jerks, and I knew that she was crying. Doug was whispering something, but I couldn't hear what he was saying.

"Let's try up on the stage," one of them said. "He's

gotta be up there, unless this one made a mistake."

"I didn't make a mistake," the boy insisted. "I seen him come in here."

Their footsteps came closer. I could feel the stage vibrate beneath me as they stepped up from the main floor.

I squeezed Cindy's arm as I stood up. "Here I am," I said, walking quickly toward them.

"Hold on there!" one of them yelled.

"Look out!" somebody else shouted. "He's got something in his hand!"

"It's a package of doughnuts," I said.

Two of them grabbed my arms, and the others surrounded me. "Keep hold of him," one man said.

"I won't run," I told them. "You think we could get out of this smelly place?"

I was led out into bright sunlight, which blinded me for a moment. The man on my right kept both of his hands firmly on my arm. The other man let go of me, but stayed close.

"It's good to breathe real air again," somebody behind me said.

"Boy, that light hurts your eyes, don't it?" said the man on my left.

"I knew I seen him go in there," the boy said.

I was hauled up the street by the whole gang. They weren't much of a posse—a fat man in an apron, several old duffers, the boy, a fireplug of a man in coveralls, and the man holding me—a tall guy in a white uniform with CARL written on the pocket.

The men talked back and forth, but nobody said anything to me. A few people looked out from doors to see what was happening, but none of them lasted very long. I probably didn't look very interesting.

We stopped in front of a small grocery store with a huge 7-Up sign in the window. A chubby Chinese man wearing a yellow apron came out of the door and said something in what I guessed was Chinese.

"Here you go, Wan Lee," the fat man said. "He was hiding down in that old movie house."

Wan Lee looked at me, took a step or two to one side, and looked me over once again. He shook his head and mumbled something. "I'm sorry," I said. "I was hungry, and I took some things to eat."

"No," Wan Lee announced. "Not the one. Not the robber. Robber got much mo' up on top." He held his hands several inches above his own hair. "Much mo'. Not like this one." He made a quick chopping motion that summed up my hair style.

"Come on, Wan Lee," the fat man said. "This is the boy. He still had your doughnuts. See?" He handed Wan Lee the package, and Wan Lee studied it for a minute.

"Not the one," he said again.

"You think maybe there was another one back in the picture show?" one of the old men asked.

"I did it," I said. "I don't know what's wrong with him. He saw me do it. I took those doughnuts. I'm sorry, but I was hungry."

"Not the robber," Wan Lee said disgustedly.

"Yes, I *am*. You know I am."

"Wan Lee, you're nuts," the fat man said. "He's telling you he did it. What more do you want?"

Wan Lee glared at me and shook his head.

"All right," Carl said, "who saw him besides Wan Lee?"

"I did," the boy said. "I followed him just as soon as I heard Wan Lee yelling. I followed him the whole way and seen him go into that theater. I told you I did."

"And this is the guy you saw, right?"

"I guess so."

"Well, was he or wasn't he?"

"Of course I was," I said. "I already told you I was."

"He's the one," the boy said, not sounding very sure.

"Not the robber," Wan Lee said. "I saw."

"You're crazy," I said.

Carl pulled on my arm. "You're the crazy one, son. If you'll just keep your mouth shut, you'll be off scot-free. You want to go to jail?"

"No, but I did it."

"So what?" Carl muttered. "Just shut up a minute, will ya?"

The men were beginning to drift away. Wan Lee was still standing in the same spot and shaking his head. "Not the one," he said to nobody in particular.

"Hey, Wan Lee," Carl said, "what if I pay you for what he took and we forget the whole thing?" Wan Lee said something I didn't catch. "What do you say? Let's get it over with. How about a dollar for the whole thing?"

"Two dollah," Wan Lee said.

"Two bucks for a twenty-nine cent package of dough-nuts? Don't give me that, Wan Lee. You don't even think this is the right guy."

"Two dollah."

"Forget it, then. I was just trying to get this thing over with. He didn't take that much stuff."

"Take many thing. Two dollah."

"Look, let's split the difference. A buck and a half, all right?"

"Dollah sixty-five."

"All right," Carl shouted. "I'm not going to fight with you for a lousy fifteen cents." He handed Wan Lee a dollar and counted some change into his hand. "All right. That's a dollar sixty-five. And you're not welcome."

Wan Lee closed his hand over the money, turned quickly, and walked back into the store. As he stopped to close the door, he turned back to me. "You not the robber," he said.

Carl still had his hand on my arm. "All right, son. I don't know whether you're the robber or not, but you owe me a dollar sixty-five, and you're going to make it good."

"I don't have any money," I said.

"I know that. You wouldn't be swiping stale doughnuts if you had any money. Come with me. I'll buy you some breakfast, and then you're going to work off what you owe me."

We went down the street to a small restaurant, where the fat man cooked eggs and bacon for me. "Feed him good, Vic," Carl said. "He'll need all the energy he can get."

I ate while Carl sipped coffee and watched me. When I was finished, he paid the check and took me down the street to a service station. "See that place?" he said. "It's mine. It's a good little business, and I like it. I got Billy working here on Sunday morning, and things are so slow he ends up working on his car, but I come down anyway because I like it around here."

"It's a nice place," I said, although it looked like every other service station in the world.

"You bet it is, son. I worked hard to get it, and I like being here. But there's one thing about this place that I can't stand." He looked at me and laughed. "You see those big old windows? You see how grimy and dirty they are? The reason they look like that is that I can't stand to wash windows. All day long I wash windshields. You think I want to wash windows while I'm resting? So whenever I can, I catch a robber and make him wash them for me. Not just any robber, though. I wait and get the robbers that want to suffer—the ones that keep yelling that they did it when everybody wants to let 'em go. When I find a guy that wants to suffer, then I know I've got somebody that ought to be washing windows. You get the picture?"

"I get it."

"All the window washing stuff is in the back closet. Some of it is still brand new."

The windows were just as filthy as he said. I scrubbed them over and over again, dumping out bucket after bucket of black, sudsy water. When I had been at it for most of an hour, Carl wandered back and looked at what I had done. "Too many streaks," he said. "Use newspapers to dry the windows. It makes a lot of difference." Then he laughed. "I know how to do it, see? I just don't put my knowledge to work. Now I think it's time for me to take a break and get some more coffee. I get all tired out just watching you."

A few minutes later a car pulled up to the side pumps, and the driver bounced out and helped himself. Then he rushed over, handed me two dollars, and drove away. I looked around and realized that Billy was in the back somewhere and that nobody was watching me. That was enough for me. I pocketed the money, dropped my sponge into the bucket, and walked quickly away from the station. I don't think I breathed until I was safely beyond the next corner.

13

For the first two blocks, I kept glancing over my shoulder. I half expected to see that little boy tailing me. Then when I was sure that I was away clean, it hit me what I had just done. (Question: What do you do to thank a guy who keeps you out of jail? Answer: You go back on your end of the bargain and then steal two dollars from him—if you're a first-class crum, that is.)

Up the street from the theater, a church service had just finished, and the sidewalk was filled with neatly dressed black people. I lowered my head and eased my way through the crowd. Most people looked away as I went by them. One little boy in a double-breasted suit stared up at me and said something to his mother. She clapped her hand over his mouth.

Two women, one wearing an enormous fur wrap, stood talking at the entrance to the alley. I stopped and stared through plate glass windows at plumbing supplies until I was sure that the whole crowd was watching me. Finally I walked past the women and past the front of the theater. A poster for a Tim Holt western still hung in one of the cases, although the glass had been broken out.

I walked on for three blocks and then made a circle. On my way back I stopped at a grocery store and bought a quart of milk, a box of crackers, and a package of cheese. The sack of groceries felt good in my arm. I had gone off a prisoner, and I was coming back free—and bringing lunch, besides. ("Hey, Tornado," I was going to say, "I thought you might be hungry.")

When I came back to the theater, the last of the stragglers from the church service were moving away. Nobody saw me as I ducked down the alley. I took one glance back at the street and yanked open the door.

"Doug!" I called. "Cindy! It's me."

There was no answer.

I called several more times, even though I knew it was useless. Then I moved around the building, looking for some sign of them—I don't even know what.

Because there was nothing else to do, I sat down on the edge of the stage and opened the sack. While I sat and munched crackers, I tried to come up with a plan. But nothing seemed real. I tried to imagine what it would be like to go home. I could picture our house and my mother, but I couldn't get any picture of my father at all.

The cheese disappeared, and then the milk. After that, I tried to go easy on the crackers, chewing each one thoroughly before starting another. But as soon as I tried to think of some kind of plan, I ended up with my mouth full of crackers again.

When the crackers were gone, I still had no plan. I knew that I had to go somewhere, but I couldn't think of any place to go except Twin Falls. If I went home—and there didn't seem to be many other choices—what could I say to my father?

Meanwhile, I sat and waited for Cindy and Doug.

I finally left the theater because I couldn't stand to sit there any longer. I wanted to see some people—anybody at all.

For a while that afternoon, I stopped at a park and watched an old man feed popcorn to a flock of pigeons. He kept talking as he spread the kernels—one or two at a time—but I could never make out what he was saying. On the next bench an old woman sat and crocheted, never looking at her hands. On another bench there were two old men, one on each end, both staring straight ahead. When the old woman got up from her bench, I took her place and rested for a while, but it wasn't much better there than in the old theater.

Later I found myself on Market Street, passing the movie theaters and camera shops and cut-rate clothing stores. I stopped at one of the novelty shops for a while, watching a plastic duck that bobbed its head and drank water. The store had chopsticks and jumping beans and ashtrays with pictures of Alcatraz. I bought a postcard with a picture of the Golden Gate Bridge on it. I figured I could just write that I was okay and send it to my mother. An hour later I threw the card away. I didn't have a pencil or a stamp, and I wasn't okay.

It was nearly dark when I got back to the theater. The streetlights had come on, and people were gathering for another church service. I went to the side door and called once, but I didn't go inside. The place just looked too black and lonely. Instead, I went back to the sidewalk and stood in the shadows, where I could keep an eye on the alley.

The church people came past me, seeming to hurry their steps when they noticed me standing there. One old man stopped and said, "Good evening, brother."

"Hi."

"Will you be coming with us to the meeting?"

"I'm kind of busy," I said.

He shook his head and chuckled. "You look real busy, all right." He took several steps and then turned back. "If you get all your business taken care of, you come and join us. Everybody's welcome."

"I'll see," I said and sarted walking in the other direction. After circling two blocks, I came back to stand in the same spot. By then, the sidewalks were nearly empty, and I could hear the sound of singing from the church, although I was too far away to catch the words.

I kept trying to decide what to do, but it's tough to decide anything when there aren't any choices. I was afraid to go home, and I couldn't think of any place else to go. I even thought of turning myself in to the police. (It was easier to picture the police bringing me home than it was to picture myself coming home on my own.)

Because it was cold that evening, I figured that the best direction for me would be south, where it would be warmer. If Doug and Cindy didn't show up by morning, I would locate a road going south and stand beside it with my thumb out. Sooner or later somebody would stop—either a ride or a cop.

I got out my map and tried to figure out which road to take. I was so busy figuring choices that Doug and Cindy were almost to the alley entrance before I saw them. "Hey," I yelled. I shoved the map into my pocket and dashed across the street.

"Oh, man," Doug said, "I thought you were long gone."

Doug ran and met me in the middle of the street, and we danced in a circle as we hugged each other. Cindy stood watching on the sidewalk. "They're gonna send the guys in the white coats after you two."

I followed Doug back to the sidewalk and said, "How you doing, Cindy?"

"Just dandy. How do you think? We've been walking all day, and we've had a jim-dandy time."

"What happened to you, Lars?" Doug asked. "Soon as you left here, we headed over that way. I couldn't go too close, but Cindy went right over there. But there wasn't a cop or anything. She finally went in the store, and the owner just said they got the wrong guy. She didn't find out any more."

"How could I?" Cindy said. "He was already looking at me funny. I know darn well he called the cops as soon as I left."

"We came right back here, figuring you'd be here. But we couldn't wait around. For all we knew, somebody might come and search the place any time."

I told them about Carl, making him sound meaner than he really was.

When I finished, Cindy snorted. "You're learning fast, Lars. A guy helps you out, so you steal his money and run out on him. You stay here long enough, and you'll be just like the rest of the people in this rotten town."

"Come on," I said. "I only did it because I was worried about you two."

"Dry up, Cindy," Doug said. "You got any money left, Lars?"

"Not much." I showed him the coins I had.

"Better than nothing, I guess," he said.

I looked at them and then at the alley. "Now what?"

Cindy moaned and stepped back. "When I was worried about you today, I forgot how you always came up with a question right when we didn't need one."

"We gotta get something to eat," Doug said. "That's first. There's a store over by the Vanguard with just one guy working at night. All three of us can go in there. You two wander around and look suspicious—you know, pick up stuff and put it down again. I'll come in a second later and stuff some things in my coat and then buy something. He'll be watching you and won't pay any attention to me."

"That's crazy, Douglas," Cindy said.

"It beats going hungry."

"Forget it," Cindy said. "Let's go to the bus station."

"What for?" I asked.

"There you go again, Clodhopper. What do you think —to watch the little buses go in and out? Just don't bug

me. We're going to the bus station so I can get us something to eat. Is that all right with you?"

"I didn't do anything to you."

"Oh, don't get your feelings hurt. I've been walking
all day, and I'm hungry and tired."

As we headed away from the theater, Doug began to
talk. "You did great today, Lars. Man, you think fast
when you have to. There you were, listening to those
guys come. And right in the middle of it, you figured out
that if they got you, they'd pretty soon see they'd made a
mistake and let you go. That was fast, Ace. And smart."

"Cut it out," I said. "You'll give me a big head."

"Don't let him get away with that, Clodhopper,"
Cindy said angrily. "He knows better. Go ahead and
make him listen to the truth. I'm sick of this pretend-
ing."

"I was there," Doug said. "I saw him in action."

"What happened," she went on, "is that Clodhopper
was ready to go to jail to save your worthless hide. And
you know it. You messed up, as usual. But Clodhopper
went ahead and took the blame, trying to save you."

"You're lucky you don't have a sister," Doug told me.
"They're hard to get along with sometimes." He laughed
quickly.

"I'd change the subject too," Cindy muttered.

The bus station was enormous—masses of people,
walls full of schedules, a tired-sounding voice calling out
arrivals and departures over the noise. "Why don't you
two go back outside?" Cindy said. "I'll meet you out in
front of those doors after a while."

Doug went straight to the door. I held back a little, not sure what she was going to do. I watched as she went up to a woman in a flowered dress. "Oh, ma'am," she whispered, her voice cracking, "could you help me? I'm in terrible trouble, and I gotta get home. I ran off with a boy. He said we were gonna get married. And now he's gone, and I'm gonna have a baby, and I gotta get home."

I followed Doug out the door, feeling a little sick. We walked down the street for two blocks, then turned around and came back. Neither of us said much. Then we stood outside the station, a few steps from the taxi stand, and watched Cindy through the window.

She worked slowly, sometimes standing in a corner for several minutes while she looked around. She usually picked older women who weren't dressed too fancy. Some of them would pat her shoulder and say things to her before opening their purses. Others would just turn aside, never really looking at her.

"I think I'll go down this way," Doug said. "Want to come?"

I shook my head. I hated the idea of Cindy begging, but I couldn't move away. I heard Doug leave while I watched Cindy talk to an old man in a cowboy hat. As I stared through the plate glass window, I suddenly realized that I wasn't the only one watching Cindy. Just on the other side of the glass, leaning against a pillar, a uniformed policeman was looking in the same direction I was.

I moved inside the doors and made my way through

the crowd, ducking between suitcases and shopping bags. The policeman was also heading toward Cindy, but he was moving more slowly. Cindy had her back to me. She had just stepped away from a gray-haired woman who was saying, "I don't feel a bit sorry for you. Sounds to me like you got just exactly what you had coming to you."

"Cindy," I said through my teeth as I moved past her, "we gotta get out of here. There's a cop coming after you."

"I'm right behind you," she said.

Threading my way through the lines of people, I circled back toward the door I had entered. I didn't dare look behind me to see how closely we were being followed. "Keep it moving," Cindy muttered. I pushed past a man with a trunk and headed for the glass doors. "He's coming after us," she said. "As soon as we hit the street, I'm gonna run. You stay and block the door. I'll see you around the corner."

As I pushed open the door, Cindy gave me a shove and leaped past me. I struggled to keep my balance, then fell when I realized that I could be more helpful on the ground. I tried to scramble to my feet, then pitched over frontward, directly in front of the door. I lay there in a ball, grabbing at my knee.

The policeman stepped over me, but there were enough curious people to block his way. I struggled to my feet, waving away any help. I limped through the door, past the policeman. He nudged me as I went by. "Tell her to stay out of here."

I turned around and tried to look surprised. "Are you talking to me?"

"You heard what I said."

I continued to limp along the sidewalk, but I knew that my performance was wasted.

Doug and Cindy were waiting for me just around the corner, standing back in a doorway until they were sure that I was alone. "Let's go eat," Cindy said.

"Maybe we could find a grocery store," I said. "We could get some—"

"Forget it, Clodhopper. This is my money, and I want to go to a restaurant and sit at a table and eat with a knife and fork. And anybody that wants to help spend my money is gonna do the same. I've had enough trashy business for one night. I'm not about to sit and eat out of a sack."

Even hamburgers were too trashy for Cindy that night. We ended up at one of those bargain steak houses that put their price on a big sign on the sidewalk.

We didn't say much until our food was gone. Then Cindy said, "That begging stuff makes me want to puke. It shouldn't, but it does. Most of those people, you tell 'em you're pregnant, they'll give you a little something. So why shouldn't they pay me just as much for behaving myself and not getting pregnant?"

"No reason," Doug said. "Too bad the cop came along."

"Too bad for you, maybe. I couldn't have stood it much longer." She turned to me. "How was your steak?"

"Good."

"Does it bother you that I had to beg the money for it? Did that make it taste any different?"

"No," I told her, trying to force a smile onto my face. "It was still a good steak."

"You're a liar, and you know it," she said quietly.

"Things are gonna get better," Doug said. "We've been through some tough times together, but things are on the way back up. You wait and see."

"Come on, Clodhopper," Cindy said. "Let's get out of here before he starts making a speech."

We walked slowly back toward the Rex Theater, in no hurry to get back inside that place. When we did go inside, the air seemed mustier than before, and the newspapers I pulled around myself were damp and sticky. I kept shifting around, even though I knew there was no way to get comfortable. (Question: Why was the second night in the theater worse than the first? Answer: On the first night, I didn't know how bad it would be. On the second night, I did.)

Next to me, I could hear Doug twisting around. "Doug," I whispered, "are you all right?"

"Don't worry about it, Ace. I'm okay."

"You sick or something?"

"Not like that. I don't know. It's just not right. Know what I mean?"

"Sort of."

"I mean, here we were, heading for Idaho. What are we doing in this rathole in Frisco? Nothing's been going right."

"It's not your fault, Doug. Things just happen."

Cindy's voice came crackling out of the darkness. "Running away was your fault. I don't know if you remember, but I wasn't the one who voted for all this. And you know darn well that Clodhopper wouldn't have come along if you hadn't talked him into it."

"We're gonna make it," Doug said. The papers rustled around him, but I didn't know he had stood up until I heard his shoes moving across the floor. "I'll be back later. I got some business to take care of."

"Douglas," Cindy shouted, "where are you going?"

"Don't worry about it. I'll be all right."

"What're you gonna do?"

"Just be cool. I'll be back in a while." He moved off the stage and out the door.

"And off he goes," Cindy said. "What do you figure he's gonna do this time?"

"Who knows? He'll be all right."

"Oh, sure. Look at what a fantastic job he's done so far."

We lay there in the darkness for a long time. I didn't have much luck getting comfortable, and I kept thinking about people I knew—teachers, neighbors, Uncle Charlie.

"Why didn't you take off today?" Cindy asked. "I figured you had. Doug and I walked all day. He was good and tired, and he was about ready to cash it in. If you hadn't been here, he would have been ready to think about Lytton by morning. But you had to hang around."

"I didn't know what else to do."

"You could always go home."

"It's not that easy."

"Come on, Clodhopper. Nothing's ever that easy. What about this? You figure staying in a hole like this and begging money in the bus station is easy?"

"Here we go again," I said. I rolled over onto my side and stared out at the darkness.

After a while, Cindy said, "You still awake?"

"Unfortunately."

"Hey, Lars, what's your mother like?"

"What kind of a question is that?"

"I just asked what your mother was like. What's wrong with that? This morning I told you all about my family. Now I want to hear about yours."

"I don't feel like talking about my family right now," I said.

"What do you suppose your mother thinks about you running away? Do you think she's really worried about you?"

"Just drop it, will you?"

"What's wrong with talking about it?"

"I just don't feel like it, all right?"

"All right. Then I'll talk. There's a girl back in Lytton. She's the daughter of the major that runs the place. Patty Binkley—you know her?"

"A little bit."

"Ever since I came there, Patty was really good to me. She let me wear her clothes. She helped me with my homework. She talked whenever I felt like talking. When I ran away, I wasn't even thinking about her. But I hurt her all the same. I know darn well that she felt really bad when I just took off that way." She was quiet for a minute. "You still awake?"

"Yeah."

"You know that guy that bought you breakfast this morning? How do you think he feels tonight?"

"Cut it out, will ya?"

"What's the matter, Clodhopper? Don't you like to think about these things? A guy gave you a break today, and you ran out on him. And your mother was probably crying a lot today. Those things are true, whether you want to think about them or not."

"I should have let that cop catch you today," I said.

Cindy laughed. "I wish I could have seen more of your crippled act."

"You didn't miss much. That cop wasn't fooled at all."

"It worked, though. You gave me a chance to get away. I didn't even say thank you, did I?"

"Nothing new about that."

"I'm saying it now. Thank you. And thank you for this morning. I owe you a couple."

"If you owe me, I'm ready to collect."

"I know. You want me to lay off the sermons, right?"

"You couldn't stop those if you tried. But at least you can quit calling me Clodhopper. Call me Eric. Or Lars. But not Clodhopper."

She laughed. "You're too easy. You get your feelings hurt way too easy."

"It doesn't have anything to do with my feelings. I just don't like being treated like an idiot."

"Even when you act like an idiot?"

"Especially then."

"All right, Lars Eric, I'll give it a try anyway. Now, do you feel like talking about your parents and how you've hurt 'em, or would you rather lie there in the dark and think about those things?"

"I don't want to talk about 'em," I said.

"It's your choice." And she didn't say another word until morning.

So I lay there and thought for most of the night.

14

Doug was there in the morning, laughing and shouting. "Come on, you two. Get up and get moving. I'll buy you some breakfast. Anything you want. You name it—steak and eggs, flapjacks. Just get a move on."

Cindy sat up and pushed the newspapers off to the side. "All right. What's going on?"

"What's going on is that I'm starved to death. Come on. Get moving. Let's go eat some breakfast."

"Where'd the money come from, Douglas?"

"Just be glad I got some, or we might get a little hungry today."

"Where'd you get it?"

"Will you get moving? After we eat, we can talk all you want. Right now I'm starving to death. I've been up all night, thinking about what I was gonna have for breakfast. So get with it, all right?"

"Answer my question first," Cindy said.

"I got a job. Now will you get a move on?"

After we finished our bacon and eggs, Doug leaned back in his chair and stretched. "I'm not as hungry as I was, but I'm sure getting sleepy."

"All right, Douglas," Cindy said, "tell us about your job."

"It's just a job, and it pays money."

"It's crooked, isn't it?"

"What kind of question is that?"

"I know it's crooked. If it wasn't, you'd say so. What are you getting yourself into this time?"

"I got a job. Don't worry about it, all right?"

"Doing what?"

"What difference does it make? I got a job, and I'm making some money, so you won't have to go back down and beg at the bus depot. We gotta eat, and we gotta buy some bus tickets. Twin Falls is waiting for us."

"I want to know what you're doing." Cindy's voice was loud enough that other people in the restaurant were turning to look our way.

"If you have to yell, let's go outside," I said.

Doug scooped up the check and carried it to the cash register. He paid with a five-dollar bill and pocketed the change. "They seem to think my money's all right," he said as we reached the sidewalk.

"Douglas, I want to know what you're doing. I know it must be crooked and stupid, or you wouldn't be acting this way. What is it?"

"I knew you'd be like this. I bring in the money we need. So what? I keep us from going hungry. So what? All you can do is complain."

"You're just stalling, and you know it."

"What difference does it make? I'm working at a parking garage—washing cars and sweeping up and things like that."

"And this garage just happens to be the one that Mallory runs, right?"

"What do you expect? Who else you think is gonna give me a job in the middle of the night? Who else is gonna help me out without asking any questions? Mallory knows I'm all right. When I got picked up, I didn't say a thing about him, and he knows it. He knows I'm safe."

Cindy shook her head, and I thought she was going to cry. "So you're just washing cars and sweeping, huh?"

"That's all I did last night. I swear it. That's all."

"What about tonight?"

"Look, you liked your breakfast, didn't you? Maybe you'd rather go back down to the bus station. I got us some money, and I'll get us some more—enough to get us out of this place. So just lay off."

"You don't want to talk about it because you know what you're doing is dumb."

"I'm too tired to fight with you," Doug said. "Right now what we all need is a hotel room. We'll take baths and sleep on beds for a change. What do you say to that? You ready for a real bed? There's a guy down at the garage that can get us a room. And we can pay the rent later. How does that sound?"

"I don't want a hotel room," Cindy said quickly. "Not if the money's coming from Mallory. If you've got some

money, you'd better hang on to it. The quicker we get out
of this town, the better I'll like it."

"Suit yourself," Doug told her. "I'm so tired right
now, I could go to sleep anywhere. Even that floor will
feel good."

Five minutes after we reached the theater, Doug was
sound asleep. I used a newspaper to clean my shoes and
then slapped the worst of the dirt out of my jacket and
pants. "Hey, Cindy," I whispered, "let me borrow your
comb."

"You don't have enough hair to matter," she said, but
she brought it to me. "What are you up to, Clodhopper?"

"I'm getting ready to look for a job. And I thought
you were going to quit calling me that."

"All right, Lars Eric, what kind of a job do you think
you'll find?"

"I don't know. I'll try anything. We have to get some
money and get out of here." She started to say something, but then shook her head. I handed her the comb.
"Thanks. I'll see you later."

"Good luck, I guess."

When I got to the sidewalk, I didn't know where to
go, except that I wanted to stay away from Carl's service
station. I headed in the opposite direction while I tried
to plan my attack.

I had never looked for a job, and I didn't know how
to go about it. Once a big grinning fellow had come to
the dairy and asked, "Do you need a good worker?"
That line had impressed me, and it seemed as good as
any.

I walked several blocks before I worked up the nerve to go inside any of the stores. I told myself that I was waiting for a place that felt right. Remembering all the story books about kids delivering groceries, I started with a small grocery store called the Buy-Rite. A short bald man stood behind the counter, smoking a black cigar. I stepped through the door and marched straight toward him, keeping my head high and my shoulders back. "You want something?" he said.

"I was wondering if you needed a good worker."

"What?"

"I'm looking for a job."

He puffed on his cigar and looked me over. "How come you aren't in school this morning?"

"I don't go to school. I graduated."

"You better go back to school, kid."

I turned and walked out the door.

The second place that felt right took even less time: "Do you need a good worker?"

"No. Sorry. Will you close that door on your way out?"

After the first few places, I quit worrying about how they felt. I just marched in and asked the first person I saw whether he needed a good worker.

For a while I kept track of how many places I had tried, but I lost count somewhere around fifty. (When the only word people say is "No," you can cover a lot of places in a hurry.)

At four thirty that afternoon I went into a diner and

asked the man at the cash register if he needed a good worker. He looked at me and laughed. "I still don't need one, kid." Then I realized that I had already been there. I figured it was time to quit.

(Question: Who said this was the land of opportunity? Answer: I don't know, but he probably wasn't a skinny fifteen-year-old in San Francisco.)

I met Cindy a half block from the theater. She handed me a sack full of groceries as I came alongside. "Here you go, Lars Eric. It was getting heavy."

"What's in here?"

"Supper. You have any luck?"

"Lots. All bad."

"I'm sorry."

"Me too. I must have tried a thousand places—stores, restaurants, service stations, anything. I can't believe it."

"I can," she said.

Doug was awake and hungry when we came in. We sat in a circle while Cindy set out the food. "There's seventeen slices of bread in this loaf and eight pieces of bologna. You guys each get three sandwiches. I get two and the extra piece of bread. And there's two oranges and a carton of milk each."

When the sandwiches were gone, we leaned back and peeled oranges. "I tell you," Doug said, "no matter what you say about California, it has one thing going for it— oranges. Back home, when we were little, about the only time we got an orange was Christmas. Man, I could eat oranges every day of my life. When I get a house, I'm gonna plant an orange tree right in my yard. And then I can pick myself an orange whenever I want one. Wouldn't that be neat?"

"Yeah," I said. I didn't tell him that there were three orange trees in the front yard of my house.

"I was thinking today, before you came back, about the kind of place I'd like to get," Doug went on. "If a guy could get a little land, he could really make it easy. I don't mean a big ranch or anything like that. But if a guy had a little land so he could grow some fruit trees and have a garden and maybe some chickens, then he'd have it made. Even if money got tight, he'd always have something to eat."

"As long as you're wishing," Cindy said, "toss in another pair of shoes for me. I'm about to wear a hole through these."

Doug stood up and stretched. "I better get going. I got work to do."

"You think maybe I could get a job there too?" I asked.

He headed for the door. "Not now, Ace. Maybe in a day or two."

"Just don't go stealing anything," Cindy shouted after him. "That's all I'm asking. Just don't get started stealing parts again."

"You worry too much," Doug yelled back. "You'll get wrinkles all over your face if you aren't careful." He pushed the door closed and hit it once.

Cindy didn't say anything for a long time. She sat in the same position and rocked back and forth. "He's gonna blow it," she said finally. "He'll start right in stealing again, and he'll get caught, and that'll be the end of it."

"Maybe not," I said.

"Oh, he'll get caught, all right. Just wait and see. And it'll be your fault."

That was too much for me. "My fault?" I shouted. "You're crazy. I went out all day and tried and tried to find a job so we could get out of here, and now everything's my fault. What do you want out of me, anyway?"

"Two things," she said quietly. "First, I want you to stop yelling."

"Maybe I don't want to. I've got feelings too. And I'm sick of being treated—" I stopped because I couldn't think of the right words.

"The second thing I want," Cindy said, "is for you to think about leaving."

"There you go again. What good would that do? The only difference would be that you wouldn't have anybody to pick on when Doug was gone."

"It might make a difference to your mother."

"Look, I can't go back home. If I leave here, I'll just have to go off by myself, and what's the sense in that?"

"What about Douglas?"

"What about him? Listen, I believe what you said about him going to reform school if we get caught. I don't want that to happen, but what can I do? If you think you can talk him into going back to Lytton, you're a bigger dreamer than he is."

"All right then. What's your answer? What do you think we ought to do?"

"I came by the Strand today—you know, that theater where we went the first day we were here. They have two John Wayne movies on. I think we ought to go see 'em."

"That's your answer to all our problems? To go see John Wayne?"

"I don't have any answers," I said. "If I can see a way to help you or Doug, I'll take it, but I don't think I can stand to sit around here all night. Do you have any money?"

"What do you mean? You ask me to go to the movies, and you expect me to pay for the tickets?"

"That's right," I said. "What do you expect from a clodhopper?"

15

After we saw the movies, I went to the men's room and scrubbed myself and even washed the socks and underclothes that I had in my jacket pocket. I wrapped the clothes in paper towels and stuffed them inside my jacket. (Question: What would I have done if someone had come in while I did my socks in the sink? Answer: One man did. I just kept scrubbing, and he didn't even seem to notice.)

Cindy was waiting for me outside the door. "It's about time you got here. I already had to chase off one weirdo."

"Sorry," I said. "I thought you were going to do your clothes too."

"I couldn't. It was like the bus station over there. I could hardly get to the sink to wash my face."

"Let's go. These things are starting to soak through the towels."

We walked along Market Street for a few blocks, not saying anything. When we reached the street where we turned, Cindy said, "Listen, Lars, I need to make a phone call. I would have made it back in the theater, but the phone there was broken."

"Who do you want to call?"

"What difference does it make?"

"Look, I'm in this too. I want to know who you're gonna call."

"All right. This afternoon I called the Salvation Army people here. They said they'd call Major Binkley for me."

"Oh, great. So they know you're in San Francisco."

"Look, I had to know. Can't you see that? I had to know if Douglas could go back to Lytton if he wanted to."

"But he doesn't want to."

"I had to know if he could. I'm supposed to call back and see what Major Binkley said."

"Go ahead. They already know where you are, anyway."

Cindy spent a long time in the telephone booth. When she opened the door, she was crying. "No good, huh?" I asked.

She dug into her purse for a Kleenex. "They'll take us back. The major says we'll be disciplined, but they won't send Douglas away just for this. And the man here says that he'll give us bus tickets if we want to go."

"So what's the matter?"

"Come on, Lars. You've seen people cry before." She managed a quick smile. "The man I talked to was so nice. I mean, he really cared what happened to us. Before I hung up, he said a prayer for our safety. And all of a sudden I was bawling. It knocked me for a loop to find somebody that treated me like I was worth something. You know what I mean?"

"Yeah, I know." I put my arm around her shoulders as we started up the street.

We had gone a few blocks when a car pulled alongside, a low-riding black Ford with flames painted on the side. Cindy and I kept walking. All I could see out of the corner of my eye were heads of wavy hair and black jackets.

One of the heads leaned out of the window. "Hey, baby, how 'bout a ride?"

"No, thanks," Cindy said, without looking at him.

The car crept along, staying even with us. "Is that your boyfriend, or are you taking a lamppost for a walk?" Several of them laughed.

Another window rolled down, and a deeper voice said, "Hey, Skinny, I want to see how fast you can run. You want to stay alive, you turn around and run back up the street. If I get hold of you, I'll turn you inside out."

"C'mon, baby," the other voice said, "you get to come to our party."

"You got three seconds, Skinny. Start running while you still can."

A lone car passed, headed in the opposite direction. Ahead of us were blocks of empty sidewalk. I glanced over at Cindy, who kept walking at the same pace. "C'mon, baby, everybody has a good time at our parties."

We passed a narrow alley, filled with garbage cans

and cardboard cartons. I looked sideways and saw that it ran through to the next street. Cindy kept walking right past it.

"Three seconds, Skinny. Starting now. One. Two."

"Back to the alley," Cindy whispered. She spun around and raced toward it. I was a step behind her. I heard a car door open, but I didn't look back.

Cindy weaved between stacks of cartons and rows of garbage cans. I stayed right behind her, holding back just far enough so that I wouldn't step on her heel. Somewhere in the dark a cat hissed as we ran past. The far end of the alley was much less cluttered, and I moved up alongside Cindy as we headed for the light.

The new street was as quiet as the one we had left. Apartment houses faced each other, and the curb was lined with parked cars. As we reached the sidewalk, I heard somebody in the alley behind us. Down the block, tires were squealing as the black Ford turned the corner. We raced away from the oncoming headlights.

Up ahead of us I saw an old man climbing the steps toward the door of an apartment building. He was the only other person in sight. He looked our way, then began to shuffle forward, reaching into his pocket for his keys.

I dashed ahead of Cindy. The Ford drew even with me, then went past before hitting its brakes. I paid no attention. I had only one goal. I had to reach the old man before he slammed that door.

He twisted the key in the lock and stepped forward, pulling his cane inside. I raced toward him as he pulled on the key. I saw the key come free and the door start to close. As I reached the stairs, I sprang upward, landing with my right foot on the middle of the steps, then diving forward toward the stoop, my hand stretched out in front of me.

My chest crashed against the cement steps as the door slammed on my wrist. I crawled forward, pushing the door open. Cindy shoved past me and eased the old man out of the way. "What's the matter with you?" he shouted.

I slammed the door as two guys started up the steps. I watched through the glass as one of them came to the stoop and began kicking the door.

"You kids get out of here," the old man said. "I'm going to call the police right now."

"Do that," Cindy said. "Get a move on."

"I will. You just bet I will." He headed toward the elevator. "And I'll tell the manager too." Cindy and I dashed down the hall past white doors with gold numbers on them.

Near the end of the hallway we saw a door without a number and pushed it open. A wooden stairway led down. "Nothing to lose," Cindy said. We stepped through the door and pushed it closed behind us. I fumbled all around for a light switch but couldn't find one. Finally we gave up and felt our way down the stairs.

Enough light came through the high windows of the basement so that we could get our bearings. The center of the area was taken up by a huge furnace, with pipes leading away from it. Along the walls were cupboards, each with a number and a padlock. We moved around the room, searching for a way out. The only door we could find was locked, and it looked solid enough to hold back a tank. Each of the windows was barred.

"Guess what?" Cindy said when we completed our circle. "We're trapped."

"We're better off than we were," I said, sitting down on the bottom step. "I wonder if that old guy called the cops."

"Probably not. But I'll bet he called the manager."

"Oh, man," I said, "it feels good to rest a minute."

Up above us, feet pounded. "Quick!" Cindy whispered. "Under the stairs." I dove away from the steps and crawled back into the darkness. A door opened, and the whole room was suddenly flooded with light. Feet struck the wooden stairs, moving slowly downward. I pushed up against the wall, trying not to breathe.

The door opened again, and a woman's voice said, "Anybody down there?"

"Nah," a man answered. "They're long gone by now. Kauffman's probably seeing things again." The footsteps went back up the stairs, and the lights went out.

"Oh, brother," Cindy said. She moved out from beneath the stairs and plopped down on the floor.

"I guess we better wait here a while," I said.

"I don't know about you, Lars, but it's gonna be a while before my legs work right, anyway."

We waited for half an hour, then crept up the stairs and into the empty hallway. We walked quickly to the front door and stood looking at the street. "Those hoods wouldn't wait this long, would they?" I asked.

"That's one of your clodhopper questions," Cindy said. We hurried down the steps and along the sidewalk, ducking into doorways whenever a car came along. None of the cars turned out to be the black Ford, but I still didn't settle down until we were back inside the old theater.

Once there, I unsnapped my jacket and pulled out the soggy bundles. I lit a match and looked at my wet clothes. "Guess what?" I said. "I lost a sock somewhere."

"If you decide to go back and look for it, you're going by yourself."

"Not likely," I said.

"Well, Lars Eric," Cindy said after a minute, "what do you think?"

"About what?"

"You're acting like a clodhopper again. What do you suppose I mean? What do you think about good old San Francisco?"

"Look, you don't have to start in. You're right. I agree with you. I'm sick of the whole stupid mess. What else do you want me to say?"

"Nothing, Lars," she said quietly. "Are you ready to go home?"

"I don't know." I tried to imagine going back to my house, but I still couldn't picture it.

"What else can you do?"

I didn't have an answer for that.

"Lars," she said after a minute, "if I can get Douglas to go back to Lytton, will you come with us?"

"He won't do it."

"That's not what I asked. If he agrees, will you come along?"

I sat there and took in the musty smells of the old building. "He won't agree, but if he did, I guess I would. My uncle Charlie would let me stay at his place, and maybe he could get things worked out."

"Why don't you just go home and work things out yourself?"

"Look, you take care of you, and I'll take care of me, all right?"

"All right, Lars."

After sitting for a while, I started moving around my newspapers, trying to get my bunk into some kind of order. When I couldn't get the papers untangled, I lit a match to see what I was doing and ended up burning my fingers before things were straightened out. Cindy was still sitting in the same place, her head bent forward. When I lit a second match, I realized that her whole body was quivering. "Are you all right?" I asked.

"Just put out that match and go to sleep."

"You're crying, aren't you?"

"So what?"

"Can I do something?"

"Yeah. You can shut up and leave me alone."

I threw aside the newspapers. "That's the trouble with you. I try to be nice to you, and you treat me like dirt. What's wrong with me trying to help you? That's what I want to know. What's so bad about that?"

"Lars," she said quietly, "come here."

"What for?"

"Just come here." I walked over and stood beside her. "Where are you?" She reached up and took my hand. "I'm sorry," she said.

I sat down beside her without letting go of her hand. "Doesn't matter."

"I started thinking about tonight and those creepy hoods, and it just got to me. You're a real runner, you know that?"

"I was following you most of the time."

She squeezed my hand harder, and I could feel her trembling. "I'm okay," she sobbed. "I'm crying, but I'm okay. I'm just glad we're safe."

For a long time we sat there in the dark, holding hands and listening to the faraway sounds of the city.

16

When I pulled myself out of the newspapers on Tuesday morning, Cindy handed me a package of cinnamon rolls and a carton of milk. "I thought you were gonna sleep all day."

"It's this great mattress," I said, biting into a roll. I looked over to see Doug sleeping. "You been awake long?" I whispered.

"Don't worry about whispering. Nothing's gonna bother him. I woke up when he came in. Seven o'clock or so. He was all beat up. Looked like he'd been run over by a bulldozer."

"What happened to him?"

"I don't know for sure. He could hardly talk. I went to the service station to get some towels to wash him off, and he was asleep when I got back. Somebody had bandaged him up, more or less, but he's a mess. I went ahead and scrubbed off the worst of the blood, and he slept through the whole thing."

"You should have woke me up."

"There was nothing you could do. Besides, you looked

so peaceful, I just couldn't do it. You were smiling in your sleep. Must have been a good dream."

"I can't remember," I said. "These rolls are great."

"Yeah. I went to that little bakery we keep passing. I figured we might as well have a good breakfast."

"Did you talk to Doug about going back?"

"He was out on his feet when he got here. But what can he say? He's so beat up, he can hardly walk, and he doesn't have any money. I know. I checked his pockets and got his last dime. I think he'll be willing to go, especially if you are."

"When do you want to go?"

"I figured to let Doug sleep for a while. We can go over to the Salvation Army headquarters this afternoon."

I finished my rolls and drained the last of my milk. "That was good. I'll be back in a while."

"I wouldn't go to that first service station. The owner chased me off when I took the towels."

"I'll be gone for a couple of hours," I said. "Maybe three."

"What for?"

"I've got something I want to do."

"Like what?"

"It doesn't matter. I'll be back before you're ready to leave here." I brushed off my clothes and ran my fingers through my hair.

"What are you up to? I want to know."

"It's no big deal. I'll be back before Doug wakes up."

"Are you ashamed of it? What's the big secret?"

"Listen, Cindy, I don't have to answer to you. I've just got something I need to do."

"You gonna buy something?"

"I might—as long as it doesn't cost more than thirty cents or so."

She smiled, but then went on. "Please, Lars. I want to know. I don't want to sit here and worry about what's happening outside."

"You can't just let it be, can you?"

"No."

"All right. I'm going back to Carl's service station and wash the windows I was supposed to wash on Sunday. I don't care if it's dumb. He's the only guy in this whole stupid city that treated me decent, and I just figured . . . Oh, I don't know. I'm just going over there and doing it."

"You're weird, Lars. You really are. You're finally going to do something smart and nice, and you're ashamed of it."

"I'm not ashamed of it."

"Oh, no. That's why you were bragging about it so much."

"I'll see you later," I said.

Carl was working on a flat tire when I reached the station. I came up and stood alongside while he continued to pull on the tube. "What can I do for you?" he said, without looking up.

"I came back to wash your windows," I said.

He glanced up quickly and then turned back to the

tire. "By golly, it's Jesse James. Came back to finish the job, huh?"

"I'm sorry about Sunday. I had to do something."

"So you figured you could come back here two days later and the dirty windows would still be waiting for you? That what you figured?"

I didn't know what to say. "I guess so," I mumbled.

Carl threw back his head and laughed. "Well, you figured right, pal. Nobody around here touched any of those windows. So you can start right in where you left off." He pulled the tube free of the rim. "Somehow I didn't expect to see you again. But you're a strange bird."

He brought out the bucket and sponges, and I went to work. I washed every window in the station, from the big plate glass jobs in the office to the small panes in the service bays. (Question: Which is more fun—milking cows or washing windows? Answer: Which is more fun —hitting your thumb with a hammer or hitting your finger with a hammer?)

When I was finished, I gathered the bucket and sponges and carried them into the office. "I'm all through," I told Carl.

"You figure we're square now?"

"Yes."

He laughed. "I don't. I figure I got the best of you by a long shot. You did a whale of a job on those windows. For a robber, you're a heck of a window washer." He studied me for a minute. "What're you going to do now?"

"I'm going home."

"Good." He reached into his pocket. "Here. I want to give you a little extra for all that work."

"That's all right," I said. "I owe you two dollars you don't even know about. Sunday a guy got gas and gave me the money."

Carl laughed again. "Know what, son? I just don't think you're cut out for a life of crime." He took out his wallet. "Let me give you a couple of dollars for some lunch. How's that?"

"That'd be fine," I said. I took the money and started away, but it seemed as if I owed him more than that. "Carl," I called back, "you're the greatest."

He laughed. "Tell it to my old lady." He waved and turned away.

Doug was just waking up when I got back to the theater. His face was scratched and puffy, and his clothes were spattered with blood. One of his hands was wrapped with gauze. "Wow," I said. "You look like you've been wrestling a wildcat."

"I don't feel that good," he said, pulling himself to his feet. "I hate to be high society, but I think I'll go wash my face."

"Go with him, Lars," Cindy said. "He looks a little shaky."

"Come on," Doug said. "You're talking about the Tennessee Tornado. You don't hear me yelling uncle, do you? I'm a little crippled up, but I'll be all right."

I went with him all the same, and he didn't seem to mind. I left him at a service station while I went on up the block to a grocery store for some bread and bologna. I came back to find a man yelling at Doug.

"Just clear outa here," the man was shouting. "That toilet's for my customers. What do you think this is—the YMCA?"

Doug headed for the sidewalk, where I was standing. "If you're going to act that way, man, I'll take my business somewhere else." He laughed.

"Beat it, wiseacre," the man yelled.

"You kill me," Doug shouted back. "Here you are worrying about a paper towel or two, and that guy working for you is shorting you fifty bucks a week."

"What's that?"

"Bye, sucker." He and I hurried down the street.

"Hey," I said, "how do you know what anybody's doing in that station?"

"Wise up, man. I don't know a thing. But that old guy'll be worrying about that for months."

We went back to the theater and ate our sandwiches. Cindy had almost nothing to say until we were through. Then she looked over at Doug. "All right, what happened to you last night? Somebody throw you off a building?"

"Crummy luck. The same crummy luck that's been fouling us up ever since we started."

"You were out stealing, weren't you, Douglas?" He shrugged. "Weren't you?"

"You know I was. What do you have to ask for?"

"I just wanted to hear you admit it. What happened? Did somebody catch you at it?"

"Almost. I had the hood of the car up, and there was

nobody around, and then all of a sudden this guy grabbed me. I spun around, and both of us fell over. I kept trying to pull loose, but he had hold of my coat. There was nothing to do but pull out my arms and run. He was yelling, and people were coming out of their houses."

"You're really something," Cindy said.

"You asked me. You want to hear the rest or not?"

"Don't stop now. How'd you get hurt?"

"They were chasing me. I ended up running through people's backyards, going over fences and through hedges. One place I went over a fence, and there was nothing on the other side but a dropoff. I slid all the way down it. I thought I was a goner."

"I can't believe you," Cindy muttered.

"The worst of it was that my car was still back on that street—the car that I got from Mallory's garage. So I had to wait for most of the night and then sneak back and get the car."

"Last night was a great night," Cindy said. "Lars and I got chased by a gang of hoods. They tried to get me in the car, then chased us when we ran off. If we hadn't been lucky, there's no telling what would have happened. No, that's not right. I know exactly what would have happened. Do you want me to spell it out for you?"

"Don't bother," Doug said.

"So look where we are. You're all beat up, and you don't even have a coat. We've been staying here in this rathole, sleeping under newspapers, begging money or stealing it. We're lucky we haven't been picked up already. We were extra lucky last night, or none of us might be here now. We're at the bottom, and we can't go on like this. Right or wrong?"

"Right," Doug said.

"So it's time to go back to Lytton. I called the Salvation Army people here, and they called Major Binkley. He said we could come back and that you wouldn't get sent to Preston just for running away. And the man here said he'll give us bus tickets. How does that sound?"

Doug looked at her and then at me. It was hard to tell what he was thinking. "Sounds like you've got it all figured out."

"So what are we waiting for?" Cindy said. "Let's gather our stuff and go. We've been in this hole long enough already."

"Suits me," I said, starting to get up.

Doug didn't move. "We made a bad mistake coming here to Frisco in the first place. People around here are rotten. They won't give you any kind of a break. Here we are—the Man from Mars and I are headed for Twin Falls. What are we doing hanging around a place like Frisco? That was a bad idea that just got worse and worse."

"Nobody's gonna argue with you on that one," Cindy said.

"The crazy thing is, we started out good. That train took us all the way to Willits. We should have figured that things were meant to be that way and just headed north from there. We could have cut over to Twin Falls after we got into Oregon. We'd be there right now."

"But we're in San Francisco, broke and dirty," Cindy said.

"I don't blame you, Cindy. If I'd been you, I would have called the Salvation Army too. You're right about Frisco. This is no place for us to be."

"You're ready to go back to Lytton, aren't you?" Cindy asked.

"Almost."

Cindy threw aside the newspapers she had wrapped around her legs and stood up. "Almost?" she said disgustedly. "What does that mean?"

"I'd go back to Lytton right now, except for one thing. Tonight—just tonight—we got a chance to make enough money to buy bus tickets to Twin Falls. Nothing to it. I need somebody to help me, but together we can make enough money so that we can leave for Idaho in the morning."

Cindy ran over and kicked him in the leg, hard enough to make him jerk back. "You're so dumb, I can't stand it," she screamed.

"Cut it out," Doug shouted. "I'm hurting bad enough as it is." Cindy moved behind him, and he turned so that he could keep facing her.

"You're crazy," she yelled. "You're sitting here looking like somebody ran you through a cement mixer, and you can't wait to go out and try again." She picked up a piece of wood and threw it in his direction.

"Cut it out," he said, talking more quietly. "I mean it. Sit down for a minute, will you? Just listen to what I have to say."

"You don't have anything to say that I want to hear."

"It won't hurt you to listen. That's all I'm asking. Just listen to what I have to say."

Cindy sighed and sat down slowly, tucking her skirt around her knees. "All right, let's hear it and get it over with."

"I got a chance to make some good money tonight," Doug said, "but I can't do it by myself. I thought I could, but I can't. You can't keep watch and get parts at the same time."

"Terrific," Cindy said disgustedly. "We can all go out and be thieves together. Is that the best you can come up with?"

I looked over at Cindy, then said, "Let's go home."

"Hey, Lars," Doug said, turning toward me, "I don't blame you. I don't care how many cows you have to milk, it can't be as bad as this place. But the whole world's not like this. We just had a bad run of luck. Now we've got a chance to turn things around. We'll get the money tonight and go to Twin Falls in the morning. If you don't like it there, you can always go home. But you ought to try it, anyway. Those cows will still be waiting for you. What've you got to lose?"

"Plenty," Cindy shouted. "What is it with you, Douglas? It's not enough to mess up your life and mine. You won't be happy until you get Lars in trouble too."

"Don't listen to her, Ace," Doug said. "If there was any danger, I wouldn't let you two near it. Look, one of you can stay at each end of the block. That's all you'll have to do. If somebody comes along, you just yell and take off."

"Let's go home," I said again.

Doug looked at me and shook his head. "I don't believe what I'm hearing, man. I know you must be feeling bad right now because you were never a quitter."

"Spare us," Cindy groaned.

Doug moved closer toward me. "How about this, Champ? Tomorrow we leave, no matter what. Does that suit you?"

I shrugged, waiting for the rest of it.

"Tomorrow morning we're out of here. If we make enough money tonight to buy bus tickets to Idaho, we'll go up there and see what that part of the world looks like. If we don't have the money, then we'll go back to Healdsburg, and I won't even argue. What do you say?"

Cindy was shaking her head, but I looked away from her and said, "I don't know."

"Come on, Lars. Give me a break. I didn't ask you for a week or even three days. Tonight's the night. If we don't have the cash for bus tickets tomorrow morning, that'll be it. We'll eat a good breakfast, kiss this place good-bye, and go back to Healdsburg."

"You don't need Lars," Cindy said quickly. "I'll be your dumb lookout. Just keep Lars out of it altogether."

"I can take care of myself," I told her.

Cindy glared at me. "There you go—acting like a dumb clodhopper again."

"Listen," I asked Doug, "we wouldn't be taking any big chances tonight, would we? Nothing crazy?"

He leaned back and grinned. "We'll play it safe, Ace. If anything looks wrong, we'll walk away. Shoot, we'll run away. If it's not a sure thing, we'll forget it."

"Then let's forget it," Cindy said.

"And this is it?" I went on. "Tomorrow we're outa this place, one way or the other?"

Cindy groaned and kicked at a pile of plaster. Muttering something, she marched to the other end of the stage and stood with her back to us.

"Don't pay any attention to her," Doug said. "She just wants to go off and pout for a while." He shoved some newspapers to one side. "Look, Ace, I'm as sick of sleeping in newspapers as you are. Tomorrow we'll be gone. And the money will decide which way we go. I won't even argue."

Cindy walked back toward us. "What a great pair you are—Tweedledum and Tweedledumber."

"What do you say, Champ?" Doug asked me. "You'll stay with me for one more night, won't you? I need your help."

"Tell him to take a flying leap," Cindy said.

I looked at Cindy quickly, then looked back toward Doug. "All right, but this is just for one night, and we're not going to take any chances."

"It's a deal," Doug said, reaching out and taking my hand. "I knew I could count on you. Tomorrow we'll be back on the Boll Weevil Express."

"I think I'm gonna puke," Cindy said.

"Come on, Cindy," he said. "Don't be a pain. What difference does one day make? If I'm wrong, the major'll take us back tomorrow." He began to straighten the papers in his bunk. "I think I better rest awhile. That's what we all should do. We're gonna be busy tonight."

I watched him lie down and cover himself with papers. Cindy walked over and sat on the edge of the stage. I stood up and started toward her.

"Get out of here, Clodhopper. I don't even want you close to me."

"Look," I said, "I just—"

"Go suck an egg." She turned her back to me.

We slept off and on that whole day. Toward evening Cindy went out for more groceries. "I'll go along," I said.

"Suit yourself."

We walked to the store without talking. Traffic was heavy on the street, and the grocery store was crowded with people picking up things on their way home from work.

We bought our usual—bread, bologna, milk, and oranges. After Cindy got her change, she ordered five candy bars. "I want us good and broke," she explained as we went out the door. "Douglas won't get any head start on those bus tickets to Idaho from me."

"He may have some money stashed."

"I took every cent he had this morning." She looked up at me. "I thought you had better sense, Clodhopper."

"What's the use of talking about it?"

"You know why you don't want to talk about it? Because you know what you're doing is dumb."

"Maybe."

"It is dumb. Really dumb. And you know it."

"I can't see any other way," I said.

"Listen to that. You've been watching too many cowboy movies, Clodhopper. Next thing I know, you'll be giving me the old one about 'a man's gotta do what he's gotta do.' But you won't be riding out with John Wayne tonight. You'll be helping stupid Douglas steal stuff and probably land us all in jail."

I didn't answer her. I was uneasy enough about the whole thing without having her go after it.

After a block or so, Cindy said, "Look, Clodhopper—"

"This morning you were calling me Lars."

"This morning you weren't acting like a clodhopper. Listen, I want you to promise me something. If you're gonna go ahead with this dumb thing, at least do this. If something happens—if we get split up or something—I want you to go back to the theater and wait at least half a day. And make sure Douglas does the same. We don't need another mess like we had on Sunday. Will you promise me to do that?"

"What's this all about?"

"Just promise me, all right? No big deal. I don't know what's gonna happen tonight. But if there's trouble, will you do what I said?"

"I guess so." I looked down at her. "You aren't planning anything, are you?"

"Come on. One idiot planner is all this bunch can stand."

17

By the time we left the theater that night, I was feeling sick. My head ached, my stomach was tight, and my knees wobbled. Doug kept talking while we walked, but I didn't have anything to say.

He left Cindy and me at a bus stop. "Just stand around like you're waiting for the bus. Nobody will pay any attention at all. I'll probably be back before the bus comes, but if you see one, just head on down the street. After it's gone, you can come back and wait again."

As we watched Doug walk away, Cindy turned to me and said, "If you had any brains at all, you'd take off in the other direction as fast as you can go."

I didn't answer her.

We stood on the curb and waited long enough to have to walk away from two buses. "Are you still glad you let him talk you into this?" she asked.

"I was never glad about any of it," I said. "I just didn't see any other way."

Cindy snorted and gave me a shove. "There you go again with that John Wayne junk. I keep telling myself you can't be as dumb as you act."

Doug drove up in an old white station wagon. The wood panels along the sides were peeling off, especially along the back fender, which had been buckled in some kind of accident. "Get in quick," Doug said, although we were scrambling in and slamming the doors.

"This your idea of a car nobody will notice?" Cindy asked.

"We've got it made," Doug announced once we were started. "With a lookout at each end of the block, I can pull right up, get what I want, and be gone in no time." I watched him as he spoke. His eyes were nearly shut, and his voice was higher and tighter than usual. I wondered if he was as uneasy as he seemed. "All you do is stand at the end of the block and keep your eyes open. Just look busy doing something. If there's a bus stop, great. If not, fiddle with your shoe—like you broke a shoelace or had the heel fall off. Nobody will be watching, but it's always better to look busy."

We traveled beside a park and then headed into an area of two- and three-story houses pushed up against each other. Doug tried to whistle but soon gave it up. "Keep your eye out for a red Buick," he said finally. "It's supposed to be along in this next block or so." We spotted the car, drove past it, and continued for two more blocks. Then Doug made two right turns and came back on the next street. "Okay, Ace," he said as he pulled to the curb, "just go down to the corner of the next block and wait. As soon as I finish and drive off, you come back up this way. Just keep walking until I pick you up."

I climbed out of the car and slammed the door behind

me, glad to be out in the open again. It was cold and windy there, with wisps of fog swirling under the street-lights. I walked along slowly, trying to look casual. (Question: How do you look casual? Answer: You think about what you feel like doing and then do the exact opposite.)

A few of the houses in that section had tiny patches of grass in front, but most had only a driveway leading to a garage. All of the windows were covered by curtains or shades. Just the same, I strolled along with my hands in my pockets and my head tilted back, trying to look like somebody out for some fresh air. Only one car passed me, and the driver didn't look in my direction.

When I reached the corner, I crossed the street so that I could get a better view of the Buick. Then I knelt down, close to the corner house, and began to work with my shoe, pulling out the string and threading it back through the holes. I was on my second shoe before Doug raised the hood of the Buick.

For a long time I just stayed on one knee and watched. Then I stood for a while, watching a pair of headlights grow larger as they moved toward me on the cross street. I wanted to scream, even though the car was still several blocks away.

As the headlights came closer, I started for the cross-walk. If the driver was planning to turn into our street, I figured I could force him to stop for a minute. Staring at the headlights, I stepped off the curb and began to limp slowly across. My timing was perfect. When the car reached the intersection, I was exactly in the center of the crosswalk, ready to yell. But the car sped past, leaving me standing there in the middle of the street. Then the hood of the Buick lowered, and Doug climbed into the station wagon. I continued across the street, no longer limping. After all the waiting it felt good to stretch out my legs and just walk. I had gone several blocks before Doug pulled alongside. "Hey, Champ," he said as I climbed in, "I told you to walk, not fly. Man, I thought for a minute you were lost or something. No problems, though. Just all free and easy. You hear that sound?"

"What sound?"

"The sound of the old cash register. Ka-ching. We're making big bucks tonight."

I looked into the back seat, where Cindy was huddled against the door. Her face was blank as it stared out at the passing lights. Except for her eyes, she could have been asleep.

Doug left us at another bus stop. "Just stay right here," he said. "I'll take this stuff to the garage and be back as soon as I can. Ka-ching. More big bucks just waiting out there."

As I watched that station wagon disappear into the fog and the dark, I felt as lonely as I ever had in my life. I tried to talk to Cindy, but each time I started, she would turn and walk away from me. The third time she turned away, I grabbed her arm. "Come on. Quit acting like this."

"Turn loose of me, or I'll scream. And don't think I won't."

I let go of her arm. "I'm sorry," I said. "I wish you'd talk."

"What do you want to talk about, Clodhopper? You want to talk about how much fun it is? You want to go all through it again, talk it all over, and get a little more excitement out of the whole thing?"

"No."

"Then what do you want to talk about?"

"I don't know."

"You're crazy, Clodhopper. You know that?"

"I know it. It's just . . ." I looked down at her, and the words began to pour out. "I just hate this whole rotten business. It makes me sick. When I left home, I figured nothing could be worse than being there—working all the time and not doing anything. But I was wrong. I didn't know about stuff like this. I don't care about going to Idaho or anywhere else. It's not worth it."

"All right," she said. "Are you ready to say that to Douglas? Are you ready to look him straight in the eye and say that?"

I reached out for her hand, but she stepped back.

"Oh, no, Lars. You can't have it both ways. If you aren't ready to face up to him, then don't come mousing around me and expect me to feel sorry for you. This is your choice. You don't have to be here unless you want to."

"I know, but—"

"Grow up, for heaven's sake. If you want something, you gotta speak up and fight for it. If you're not ready to fight, then don't come whining to me." She turned and walked away from the bus stop.

"Cindy, come on."

THE BOLL WEEVIL EXPRESS /// 195

"Don't bother me."

"Look, we can talk, can't we?"

"First you talk to him. Then we can talk. You tell him you're tired of having him lead you around by the end of your nose. Then we'll talk all you want."

She turned away from me and leaned against a building. I started to talk once or twice, but she just twisted farther away. Giving up, I wandered over and leaned against the lamppost. A Chinese man wearing a dark suit came and stood on the sidewalk halfway between Cindy and me. Each of us looked in a different direction —three strangers waiting for a bus.

When the bus came near, I checked my watch, then hurried down the street. Cindy went in the opposite direction. The Chinese man didn't glance at either of us as he climbed onto the bus. After a minute I came back to the lamppost, and Cindy came back to the wall.

Two more buses passed before Doug came back, driving a blue Ford sedan this time. Cindy and I climbed in, and he drove away quickly. "They figured it was a good idea to switch cars," he said. "Suits me. This one's a lot easier to handle. That other thing was like driving a tank."

Cindy reached forward and punched my arm. "Doug," I said, catching him between sentences.

"What's the matter, Ace?"

"I'm through with this stuff."

He laughed. "Me too. After tonight, I quit."

"I mean right now."

"Look, man, this is tough on all of us. Just hold on a

little while. Think about the big bucks coming into the cash register. Ka-ching. Look out, Twin Falls. We're coming your way."

"I don't want to go to Idaho that bad," I said quietly.

"Hey, you worry too much. You're not gonna get caught. You're just a little spooked right now. It's okay, Ace. It'll pass."

"I may be spooked," I said, my voice getting louder, "but that's not the problem. Can't you see how crummy this is? Look at what we're doing. We take the parts off some poor guy's car. He comes out in the morning, and he's stuck with a car that won't run. It's—"

"Cut it out," Doug shouted. "You expect me to feel sorry for some Frisco creep? Look, just hold on. We'll be in Idaho before you know it."

"I'm all finished," I insisted. "I'd rather go back home than do any more of this."

Doug pulled the car to the curb, stopping in the shadows. Then he turned to face me. "What is this? You said you'd stick with me. Just one night I need your help— and you gave me your word. Now all of a sudden you want to back out."

"He's starting to wise up," Cindy said.

Doug looked back toward her and shouted, "You shut up. This is between Lars and me."

"I don't count, I guess," Cindy shouted back.

Doug sagged down in the seat and didn't move for a minute or two. When he finally spoke, his voice was soft and sad. "I don't know what to do, Lars. I figured I could count on you, and now I'm up a stump."

I stared straight ahead, wishing things were different.

"What do you want, Ace? You want me to beg? Okay, I'm begging you. Help me out tonight. Just tonight. Then we'll kiss off this town and be gone. This'll be it."

"Until the next time," Cindy said.

"Shut up, Cindy!" he shouted.

"It's the old just-this-once business, Lars," Cindy said. "He's good at it."

Doug turned around in the seat and faced her. "I'm telling you to shut up," he shouted. "If I have to throw you out, I'll do it."

"You would, too," she muttered.

"You better believe it," he said as he turned toward me. "Hey, Lars, you want to take a walk? Just you and me? She can sit right here in the car. We can talk things over without her butting in."

"We can talk here," I said.

"Whatever you want, Ace. You just gotta see the way things are. Look, man, we're a team, right? The Man from Mars and the Tennessee Tornado. We started this thing together, and we stuck together. You don't want to run out on me now."

"But it's—"

"I need you this one time. Will you do that much for me? Come on. We're just a few blocks from there. I know you don't want to. I know you hate it. But I'm asking you to do it for me."

All along I thought I was going to say no, but just then I couldn't get the words out.

"Even if you think it's dumb and wrong, I'm asking you to do it for me."

"All right," I said quickly. "Let's get it over with."

"You never learn, Clodhopper," Cindy moaned.

Doug put the car in gear and pulled away from the curb. "You're okay, Champ. I knew you'd come through."

I was too mixed up to say anything. I felt as if I had no choice, but I felt like a sucker at the same time. Above everything else, I wanted that night to end.

The car we wanted, a blue Oldsmobile, was sitting beneath a small tree, only half a block from a well-lighted boulevard. "Perfect," Doug said as we drove past. "It's good and dark under that tree."

"If I'm gonna do this stupid thing," Cindy said, "I want the lighted street. I don't want to be hanging around in the dark again."

We left her at a service station on the boulevard, a block away from the street where the Oldsmobile sat. After making a slow circle of several blocks, Doug left me at the other corner and headed down the street. I watched as he pulled into a driveway and climbed out of the car.

I crouched down just beyond the corner, where I had a good view, and began to fool with my shoestrings again. The street was quiet. In a place or two, I could see the blue light of a television set through the curtains, but most of the houses were dark.

At the far end of the block, Cindy was standing on the corner diagonal to mine. She was facing away from me, her skirt flapping in the wind. Traffic on the boulevard was light—mostly trucks. The hood of the Oldsmobile was up by then, and I could spot Doug only because I knew exactly where to look.

I began to count aloud, whispering the numbers. The counting was partly to pass time and partly to keep me from thinking about what was happening. It didn't work very well in either case.

Then Cindy screamed, "Run, Douglas! Run for it!" I stayed crouched on the ground, too surprised to move, as a police car turned the corner from the boulevard into our street. Red lights blinking, the car skidded to a stop beside Cindy, and a policeman leaped out. Doug came racing up the sidewalk toward me, bent over double to stay below the level of the cars at the curb. I saw the cop standing next to Cindy as I turned and crawled around the corner. As soon as I was out of sight, I stood up and ran.

I dashed to the next corner and turned left onto a steep, narrow street. I ran uphill for two blocks, then took a side street that led past dark houses. As I slowed to a walk, I could hear Doug's footsteps echoing against the buildings. He reached my street, spotted me, and hurried forward.

"Oh, man," he moaned, grabbing my shoulder. "This time I really did it."

We walked several blocks, turning at almost every street. As we moved along, Doug groaned and swore at himself. I don't think I said anything at all; I was too scared and empty to talk.

We came over a rise and found ourselves on a street of huge old houses. Doug stopped and leaned against an electric pole. "I don't know what to do," he said. "My sister's—" His voice caught, and he stopped. "My sister's in jail, and it's all my fault, and I don't know what to do."

"I knew better," I said. "I knew better, and like a dummy, I went ahead just the same."

Doug kicked the pole once. "I don't know what to do. My whole life is so rotten. Everything just gets worse and worse." He started along the sidewalk, then stopped beside a flight of cement steps and sat down.

"You think we ought to stop here?" I asked him. There was a streetlight directly overhead, which lit up the steps like a stage.

"What difference does it make? Let 'em pick me up. The whole thing is a big sick joke anyway. I just don't care what happens to me anymore."

Right then I didn't care much either. I sat down on the steps beside him and stared at the empty street. When a car drove past, we didn't even move.

We sat there for a long time without saying a word. Every time I saw a pair of headlights, I was sure the police were coming. And I didn't really care. The only person who ever noticed us, though, was a man walking his dog, and he said hello.

Finally I grabbed the handrail and pulled myself up. "I guess we might as well not sit here all night."

"What difference does it make?"

"Not much, I guess."

Doug stood up and faced the street. "What do you think?"

"No use going back that way," I said.

"That's for sure. Let Mallory try to find that car for himself." He headed downhill.

"Hey, you got a dime?"

"Why?"

"I was thinking back there. I'm gonna turn myself in. I'll tell them the whole thing was my fault. Then maybe they'll let her go."

"I don't know, Doug."

"Why not? I don't care what happens to me. I'm not gonna let her get sent off to some jail because of me. Maybe if I talk to 'em, they'll let her to go back to Lytton. She'll be all right there, anyway."

"It just seems—"

"If you have a better idea, let's hear it."

I shook my head. "I don't have any ideas at all."

"Then let's find a phone. Right now the only thing I care about is Cindy."

As we started downhill, I remembered how Cindy had made me promise to go back to the theater and wait if something happened. It seemed useless to do that now, but it was something to hold on to.

"Hey, Doug," I said, "let's go back to the theater, just in case she got away or something. If she's not there, you can still call the cops. But we ought to check the theater first."

"Man, he had her cold."

"I know, but you know Cindy. She just might talk her way out of it."

Doug looked over at me. "You think there's a chance?"

"You know what a talker she is."

He almost smiled. "Yeah. You know, you just might

be right. When it comes to Cindy, a guy can't ever be sure."

So we walked back to the theater. It took us over two hours, but some of that time was wasted in a bunch of dead-end streets.

Doug's mood shifted every few blocks. For a while he would be saying things like "That Cindy, she's something. She could talk her way out of anything. Remember how she did in Willits? She'll be okay." Then, for no reason, he would get quiet for a while, then start talking about how we were wasting our time. "It's no use dreaming. She's in jail right now, and I'm the one who put her there." But five minutes after that, he would be saying that there was always a chance, especially with somebody as smart as Cindy.

My mood didn't change very much. I just felt empty and hopeless. And guilty—knowing that I could have prevented the whole thing and didn't.

As we came closer to the theater, both Doug and I began to walk faster. Neither of us said anything; we just picked up our pace a little more with each block. When we passed the church, we broke into a run.

We raced down the alley and yanked open the door. "Cindy!" Doug shouted. We stopped to listen, but there was no answer. I pulled the door shut slowly, and we made our way to the stage. "See, Ace?" Doug moaned. "I told you she wouldn't be here."

18

I don't know if we slept that night. I lay down among the newspapers, but whenever I closed my eyes, I kept seeing that cop leap out of the car. Doug and I talked now and then, saying the same things over and over. He was ready to turn himself in, and I wanted him to hold off until morning. "Give her until eight o'clock. A few hours won't make any difference. Just wait until eight o'clock."

When sunlight began to show through the hole in the ceiling, Doug stood up and walked back to where we kept the few things we didn't carry in our pockets. "I think I better shave. If I look okay, they're more likely to believe what I tell 'em."

When he was finished, I looked over at him. "Now what?" I asked.

"No use hanging around here any longer. It's time to go call the cops."

I got to my feet and gave the newspapers a final kick. "All right. Let's go do it."

"Hey, Ace, this is my phone call, not yours. You go

on home. There's no sense in you being in on any of this. You didn't do anything."

"Come on," I said. "I'm not about to run off and leave you."

"Hey, man, you better start using your head. This is no hero stuff. I'm just trying to save my sister." His voice caught for a minute, and he looked away. "If I can help her, I don't care what happens to me. But you can't do anything for her. All you'll do is foul things up for yourself. And maybe for us too. So come on. Let's move out of here. Get all your stuff, and we'll go."

"You sure?"

"I'm giving it to you straight, Lars. If I thought it would help Cindy, I'd take you to jail with me. That's the truth. I'd do anything to help her. But there's no way you can help."

"All right, Doug. I'll walk as far as the phone booth with you."

"Thanks, Champ." He put his arm around my shoulder as we walked to the door.

Doug shoved the door to the side and stepped into the alley. I followed, squinting against the bright sunlight. Then I stopped and stared. Cindy was standing in the middle of the alley, her hands on her hips. Doug ran toward her while I stood and watched, unable to move —just the way I had been when the police came the night before.

"All right, Douglas," she shouted, "have you had enough?"

"Yeah," he said, throwing his arms around her.

She put her hands on his chest and pushed him back. "Really? Do you mean it?"

"I mean it."

"Oh, thank God," she said, and put her arms around his neck.

They danced around the alley, laughing and hugging each other. I finally managed to come up the alley to where they were. Cindy reached out a hand and squeezed mine.

"What happened?" Doug asked finally. "How'd you get away?"

"It was awful," she said, still hanging on to him. "They kept asking me questions, and I didn't say anything. I just didn't say a word. Then they started doing things to make me talk—calling me names, yelling at me. It just went on and on. They kept doing more things. I don't have to tell it all, do I?"

"No," Doug said quickly.

"Let me tell you the last part, and then I don't ever want to talk about it again. They finally took me to a hospital to get me checked over. This nurse took me into a room, and when she turned her back, I walked right out the door. I ran down the hall and went out the first exit I saw. And then I spent the rest of the night trying to find my way back here. Now it's water under the bridge, and I don't want to go through it ever again. Can we do that, Douglas? Can we just forget the whole thing?"

"Suits me," Doug said, tears forming in his eyes. "I'm just glad you're all right."

Cindy let go of him. "Cut it out, or you'll have me bawling too. I mean it—cut it out." She took a long breath. "All right, Douglas. There's a Major Ames waiting for us at the Salvation Army headquarters. He'll give us breakfast and bus tickets. Are you ready to go?"

Doug looked over at me and shrugged. "What do you say, Ace? You figure those Healdsburg women have suffered long enough without us?"

"He has a ticket for you too, Lars," Cindy said.

"I don't have anything else going this morning," I said.

It was late afternoon when we reached Healdsburg. I looked out the bus window at the familiar sights—Lonnie's Café, Wittke's Truck Stop, the lumber yard, the ice plant. And coming along the sidewalk was old Mrs. Tankersley. I waved at her, even though I knew she wouldn't see me.

Doug leaned across the aisle and said, "I thought maybe they'd have a parade for us, but I guess we surprised 'em."

At the depot the driver announced that we would be stopping for ten minutes. Cindy stood up quickly. "I'm going in and comb my hair. It's my last chance to have a mirror all to myself."

"Gotta make a phone call," I said, and hurried after her.

As I headed for the booth, I was planning to call Uncle Charlie. He only lived about three miles from the Lytton stop. But then I glanced at my watch and realized that it was five minutes after four. My father would be sitting at the kitchen table, drinking his tea before he went to the barns.

I stuck the dime in the slot, hesitated after dialing the prefix, and then dialed the number I knew best. My mother answered the phone, as I knew she would.

"Mother," I said, "this is Lars."

"Lars, where are you? Are you all right?"

"I'm fine."

"It's Lars," she shouted, then asked again if I was all right.

"Mother, I'm fine. I want to talk to Father."

"You sure you're okay, Lars?"

"I'm fine. Really."

"He says he wants to talk to you," she shouted.

I set my jaw and waited for my father's voice to come booming into the receiver. I could hear him saying something as he came across the kitchen. "Where are you?" he yelled into the phone. "What's the matter with you—running off this way?"

I had to hold the receiver in both hands, but I managed to get my words out. "Father, I want to ask you something."

"I'll ask you something. What do you think you're doing? Huh? Running off and your mother crying and worrying. That make you happy? That what you want?"

"Father, I want to ask you something."

"What are you talking about? What do you want?"

My voice caught the first time, but I tried again. "Father, do you want me to come home?"

"I don't know what got into you. Running off, scaring everybody, causing all kinds of problems."

"Do you?"

"What are you talking about?"

"Do you want me to come home?"

"Your mother hasn't slept all week. Up all hours. Wondering where you were. Thinking maybe you were dead or something."

"Do you? Yes or no?"

"Well, goodness sake, of course I do. What do you think I'm saying?"

I wanted to stop there, but I knew that there was more to say. I bit my cheek and said, "Father, if I come home, things can't be like they were before."

"I know. I know. I been hearing about it all week from your mother. No more going to your room and checking on you."

"I'll do the milking, and I'll do my homework, but once in a while I need to go places."

"You want to run the farm, too? You run off and scare everybody, and now you want to be the boss, too? You think you can run off, and then everybody'll get down and kiss your feet, huh? That's the way you figure it, huh?"

I bit my cheek again. "No, Father. I know who's boss. But sometimes, on weekends, I need to go places."

"Okay. Okay. You sound like your mother and your uncle. So you come home, you hear? No more of this stuff."

"All right, Father. I'll be there in a couple of hours. I have to go now." I put the telephone down quickly.

As I headed back to the bus, I realized it had been

years since I had talked that long to my father. The driver glanced at me quickly when I passed, and an old woman looked at me and shook her head. I was sitting in my seat before I figured out that tears were pouring down my cheeks.

Doug leaned across the aisle and said, "Hey, Ace, it's not that bad. It's the same boring town it always was, but there's no use crying over it."

I waved him away and wiped my cheeks. "I'm all right."

"I've been thinking, Lars. As long as we're coming back here, we might as well have a little fun. I'll probably be grounded for a month or so, but you know Melody Young? I think I ought to go out with her. You can take her friend Patty. What do you say?"

"I may be grounded longer than a month."

He laughed. "Me too. But as soon as we're clear, they're first on the list. Unless I decide to go for Amy Buford.'"

"She's going steady."

"She may not be in a month. Especially if she finds out she has a chance for a date with the Tennessee Tornado."

Cindy came back to the bus, and the driver started the engine. She sank down on the seat beside me. "'You get ahold of your uncle, Lars?"

"I called my father instead. I'm going home."

"Good. How was he?"

"Mad. What else? Things are going to be all right, though."

"You sound like Douglas." She glanced back across the aisle to where Doug was looking out the window. "One favor," she whispered. "Okay?"

"Sure."

"Just don't ever tell Douglas that I said for you to go back to that theater if something happened. All right?"

"I won't say anything." Then it hit me. "You called those cops, didn't you? When we let you off by that service station, you called the cops. I don't know what you told them, but you got them there in a hurry. And they weren't after you at all."

"If you're so smart, how come you ran away with us?" she said quietly.

"But that's what happened, isn't it?"

She put her hand on my arm. "Just don't spoil things, okay?"

"Not me. It's water under the bridge. Isn't that what you called it?"

She looked at me for a long minute. "I guess you hate me, don't you, Lars—the way I messed up your plans and all?"

"There it is," Doug called, pointing ahead at the buildings of Lytton Home.

I smiled at Cindy. "Come on. You know I don't hate you. Maybe I should but I don't." I wanted to say more than that, but Doug was looking across the aisle at us.

"You know what I'd like," Cindy said quickly.

"What's that?"

"I'd like to go to Playland with you again—when we have money and aren't running away or anything."

"It'll be awhile," I said, "but it's a date."

"I can wait," she said, and headed down the aisle.

We got off the bus and then stood and watched it disappear around a turn. Then we crossed the highway and stopped once more.

"Here we go again," Doug said, turning toward the gates.

"It'll be nice to sleep in a bed and take a bath," Cindy said.

Doug laughed. "I may have to get me some newspapers and tuck them in with me. Otherwise I might not be able to sleep."

"See you in history class," I told him.

"Don't look so sad, man. We've got all those women waiting for us."

"Good-bye, Lars," Cindy said. She put her arms around my neck, pulled my head down, and kissed me quickly. I stood there, too surprised to move, as they walked away from me.

Then I turned and began my six-mile walk home. With all I had to think about, I wouldn't mind the distance at all.

About the Author

P. J. PETERSEN was born in Santa Rosa, California, and grew up on a farm in Sonoma County. He attended Stanford University, San Francisco State University, and the University of New Mexico, from which he holds a doctorate in English. He lives with his wife and two daughters in Redding, California, where he teaches English at Shasta College.

This is P. J. Petersen's third novel. His first two novels, *Would You Settle for Improbable?* and *Nobody Else Can Walk It for You*, were also published by Delacorte Press. *Would You Settle for Improbable?* (also available in a Dell Laurel-Leaf edition) was named an American Library Association Best Book for Young Adults.